I0667808

DOWN AND DIRTY

TRAYVON D. JACKSON

PENTALK PUBLICATIONS, LLC

COPYRIGHT

Text Shan to 22828 to stay up to date with new releases, sneak peeks, contest, and more...

WANT TO BE A PART OF THE TEAM?

To submit your manuscript to Shan Presents, please send the first 3 chapters and synopsis to submissions@shanpresents.com

SYNOPSIS

Down & Dirty

Not every lion roars in the lethal streets of Brick City – Newark, New Jersey. The murder rate is the tremendous, and the heroin distribution is "Hail King," D'Shawn and his two cousins, whose specialty is hotwiring cars for the exchange of money at the chop shop, finally get a chance to venture into the dope game at the grimy hands of deception and extortion. Set with a prestigious name, envy, hatred, and betrayal comes as quick as lavishness. Transparently, D'Shawn sees how dirty the game gets, all for money. But what does love have to offer, when it seems forbidden? Falling for an angel, he experiences love's true value. Skepticism inflames his heart, and makes him wonder: Was love a precious diamond, or a cardinal sin to a man engrossed in the street life? If love cries mercy, can death cry for love?

Enjoy the tale of love, loyalty, and betrayal. You thought there was closeness until she came at your throat.... The game.

Subtitle: "Cutthroat to The Last Dime"

Novel by: Author: **Trayvon D. Jackson**

WISDOM

To know something, you must go through something, and to grow, you must know what it's like to lose. Love comes in many forms, like death you'll never know who it'll chose.

Author Trayvon D Jackson

DEDICATIONS

I'll like to dedicate this to my mother Frankie Mae Jackson, my father Johnny H. Miley, my beloved sweet grandmother Jessie Mae Johnson and to my ride or die, without you I couldn't see the stars Latoya Maye, let's be successful.

VARSHAY AWOKE to the soft rapping on her window, already knowing whom the late-night visitor was. When she looked at the digital clock illuminating on her nightstand, she saw that it was 2:45 AM. *Damn why you so late, boy?* She wanted to know as she emerged from her queen size, comfortable bed. Varshay was a young Lisa Raye lookalike at seventeen years old. She was five-foot-five and developed like a thirty year old. She put to shame women twice her age and even had envious foes amongst her in society, mainly from the "Dime Piece Diva's" themselves. She was the only girl, and her only brother and the eldest, Boo, was locked away, serving life in prison at the age of twenty five.

The soft raps on the window came again persistently, before she made it over to open it up in just a short t-shirt that stopped at the base of her succulent, large buttocks, and a fish net thong. Varshay quietly eased up the window after unlocking it, and allowed her boyfriend to crawl inside. When he was inside furtively, she eased the window down partially, and enjoyed the early AM breeze. She instinctively listened to her surroundings in her home to make sure that nothing had triggered her parents to awake from their sleep. Though they slept a distance out of earshot, on the other side of the spacious, opulent home, gingerly she had to play it safe. If her father found out what she was doing under his roof, she couldn't imagine how things could turn out. When she heard nothing, like the usual, she engaged Pandora on her iPad, and let the Monica's song "Love All Over Me" emanate from its speakers. Varshay climbed on top of her boyfriend, who laid sprawled across her bed and began to kiss on his lips.

"Why you so late?" she whispered to him.

"You know I got to get this money, or your ass won't have shit for your birthday," he said in a whisper, while caressing Varshay's smooth ass.

"Yeah whatever," Varshay retorted, impishly turning her lips up in a pout, and rolling her eyes.

"Don't look like that... you miss me?"

"Yes, I do baby," Varshay retorted, kissing her boyfriend's lips again passionately, simultaneously unfastening his Polo belt and jeans.

When she felt his fingers fondling her throbbing clitoris, and inside her sultry mound, she moaned out to him breathlessly, full of anticipation of wanting to feel him inside her, like he was almost every other night.

"Baby!" she exclaimed, breathlessly. Together they slid down his Polo jeans and briefs, then guided his erected penis inside of her tight, wet love tunnel.

"Uhh!" Varshay softly moaned out gyrating her hips, rhythmically, stimulating her clitoris at his steady penetration. He spread her yellow ass cheeks apart and simultaneously pumped in and out of her. Her moans that intensified were muffled by the blanket, that she'd stuffed in her mouth. And all that could be heard over the iPad playing Monica, was the sweet sound of him penetrating her excessively wet pussy. She had an odorless smell to her pussy that he'd became obsessed with. He loved her, despite the many women he had, and she loved him for being her true love, and only love. He knew beyond skepticism she wasn't involved with any other man. He was the first man to break her virginity, and the only man in her life.

"I love you, uhh, bae!" Varshay moaned rapturously in a whisper as she came to an orgasm.

"I love you too," he said as he exploded inside her. "Ahhh!" he exhaled.

Dammit, I love this bitch! He thought, meaning every word.

CHAPTER 1
BRICK CITY (NEWARK, NEW JERSEY)

"Yo roll up that swiss, so we could kill time B," said Leon to his cousin D'Shawn, who was his older cousin and role model.

"Nigga, yo' fat ass always trying to burn without Lee... let's wait until he come back," D'Shawn replied, referring to Leon's brother, who was hotwiring a Dodge Durango further down the street from them. Lee and Leon were twins, eighteen years old, and reputable head bussers in east Newark, New Jersey, known as Brick City. They both were a chocolate complexion that was immaculately flawless, and attracted women like honey and bees. He weighed 185lbs on the stocky side, developed from the innumerable counts of times he'd been incarcerated. D'Shawn was a Tyrese Gibson lookalike, who sported a low boy fade haircut that accentuated his naturally groomed waves, that drove women insane. He also had a reputable notorious name in the streets of "East Newark, New Jersey". He was a head busser that had fear in many nigga's hearts. He couldn't count the number of females he'd had in his life. And was lucky to be fatherless at the age of twenty-one years old.

"There he go right there. Let's go!" Leon exclaimed, simultaneously making a dash toward the stolen cherry red Durango that his brother Lee was driving. Leon was stubby and short, distinctive from

Lee, who was on the stocky side and stood identical five-feet-six-inches with his brother. D'Shawn, seeing Lee artistically splack a whip always was intriguing to him. As Leon hopped in the back seat, D'Shawn took the wheel, after Lee climbed over to the passenger side.

"So, where we going first?" asked Lee while he engaged the Bluetooth system on his iPad, allowing Drake to emanate thorough the Durango's speakers. "East Orange, to go see Skip and them hoes Trina and Monique."

"Don't Monique have a sister?" Leon asked D'Shawn, cutting him off.

"Yeah, that bitch fat back there too. Here light up the swiss fat boy, and let's fog this shit out," D'Shawn said removing the blunt from behind his ear and tossing it back to Leon in the back seat.

All the trio did was steal cars and take them to a chop shop on 21st and Tango to sell them to an Arab connect at half price. It always depended on what type of car it was, and its luxurious material. Despite having no job and slowly seeing numbers in the splacking game, D'Shawn had other things in mind.

We need our own shit to lock down the Brick, D'Shawn thought as he exhaled the purple haze smoke from his mouth and nostrils. D'Shawn gingerly maneuvered through traffic on his way to East Orange, NJ, praying for no unexpected visitors like 5-0.

Inside the gambling house on 151st and Spruce, the atmosphere redolently smelled of purple haze. At a long Oakwood table sat five other poker players, who ordinarily gambled every weekend together. Some drank on Remy while some preferred malt liquor 40's. Skip hid his elation behind his poker face, when he saw he had an undefeated hand. He decided to milk the pot.

It's time to make these niggas pay, Skip thought as he awaited the four other players. When he saw that they were still fishing for a hand worth sticking around, he raised the pot.

"I raise.... 300," Skip calmly said, then took a swig from his bottle of malt liquor 40. Everyone around the table looked at Skip, knowing his technique of hitting low to high. He was the youngest amongst them and a champion poker player.

"This nigga bluffing, y'all!" Exclaimed an old school cat named, Borack.

"Well, you know how it goes. If I'm bluffing raise, and see if I follow... Or fold," Skip said.

"Oh damn, I fold," an ol'school cat named BB said, folding his hand in unison with the other prudent contenders. Leaving Borack and Skip alone to battle amongst themselves was everyone's smart move.

"You have two draws to catch up," Skip retorted.

"Oh yeah, well, I draw," said Borack, discarding his one card to receive another one from the deck.

"I raise again," Skip said, challengingly. "300 more," he retorted."

"I back raise again... 600 more," said Borack, placing $600 on the pile of money stacked neatly in the middle of the table, being handled by BB who was the cut man today. When Skip stood with his entire hefty wad in his hands and put it on the pile of money, Barack knew that he had no win.

"$1,200, all in," Skip exclaimed.

"Show your hand nigga...I fold." Borack surrendered, "Good move, Borack," Skip said, as he laid down four aces in all suits, and a spade of king. Poker Ace's," Skip said grabbing the enormous pot of money. "Lucky ass nigga," said Borack said shuffling the deck of cards for another hand.

"Skip done for the day... I'll catch y'all old heads later," Skip told everyone, grabbing his 40 malt liquor off the table and adjusting his snapback Jet's hat on his head.

Despite Skip being twenty-two, he was the youngest among them all and meekly. East Orange was the most lethal section in New Jersey, takin' the murder rate from Newark. And Skip, who was a major contributor to the statistics in the drug distribution on the East Coast, had respect from every hood. Coming outside the gambling house, meeting the ardent sun, he saw his rival homie D'Shawn hopping out a conspicuous cheery red Dodge Durango, already knowing that it was a stolen whip. Skip was ready to put D'Shawn on, but the nigga was always being a hot boy. And to Skip, that was taking a risk, something that Skip couldn't bring under his wing. Skip was an elegant five-foot-eight, 151lbs pretty boy, with a brown flawless skin complexion. He resembled Chris Brown in the face, and had a frame like Tyga from Cash Money Records.

As he walked to his black-on-black Range Rover, he observed D'Shawn and his cousins macking with Monique and Trina across the street.

I gotta sit down with D'Shawn and see where his head at fo' real on this money, Skip thought. Monique and Trina were two home girls who were in their senior year in high school, and had a fetish for any nigga that could bring forth a hundred-dollar bill. Sad to say, they were two ingenious young prostitutes. When Skip started up his Range Rover, his loud system immediately emanated from the four twelve-inch speakers booming thunderously in the rear, that was riveting to everyone in the vicinity. Skip jumped back out the Range Rover and let Meek Mills new hit scream throughout the whole block. No doubt it could be heard blocks away, the nigga had a raw ass system.

"Yo D'Shawn, leave them butter head hoes alone and come holla at me, B!" Skip yelled out to D'Shawn, simultaneously sparking up a purple haze blunt.

As D'Shawn strutted from across the street, Skip saw the looks on Lee and Leon's faces and knew how close the trio was. *What you do for one, ya gotta do fo' all,* Skip thought and called out to Lee and Leon. "Yo Lee and Leon, check it too!"

"So what's good with tonight?" Lee asked Monique who was in some black enticing booty shorts that accentuated the plump mound between her legs, and a sports bra that concealed her perky tits. Her ghetto fabulous booty left a lot of men mesmerized.

"Nigga, you talking 'bout tonight, when you get that bank up, then fuck with da girl," Monique said laughing as she walked off with

Trina, who was well-dressed in her hoochie mama clothes and bad as hell, too. Both of them had a flawless ebony skin complexion, and a Colgate smile.

"Man, fuck them dirty ass hoes B, I bet them hoes feed dirty too," Leon said, exiting the Durango to go see what Skip had on his mind.

"What's good Skip, you done circled them old heads again," D'Shawn exclaimed while clapping hands with Skip.

"Always. Shit, y'all tell me. I know that's a stolen whip y'all in. When is y'all niggas gonna lay the splacking down and get with the stacking?" Skip addressed them all.

"Man, the dope game ain't promised for us man, ain't nobody about to put us on. So, we doing us B, feel me!" D'Shawn spoke for all.

"Man, how much the Arab giving y'all for that whip?" Skip asked the trio.

"Fifteen hundred," D'Shawn retorted, speaking for all again. Being that he was the eldest, and folks ran to him first to calm Lee and Leon's impishness.

When everyone saw what Skip pulled from his pockets, a hefty wad of cash, they all went to wonderland, perplexed. The trio watched Skip peel off thirty hundred-dollar bills and hand it to D'Shawn.

"B, what's this fo'?" D'Shawn asked bemused.

"It's fo' all y'all to get in, and what y'all could have in one day. The game is free and is meant to be soaked up, prudently. After today, splacking shouldn't even be on y'alls mind," said Skip, walking back towards his Range Rover, then getting inside leaving the trio indecisive for a moment. The trio quickly got inside, and prepared to learn something most definitely new.

Skip had a nice luxurious crib outside East Orange gutters, in a wealthy mid-class neighborhood called Tanglewood. And that's where he brought the trio, who were intrigued by the opulence of Skip's home. He was eager to show the trio how he made his money, without being a hot boy. "What I'm 'bout to show y'all three is only one time. This right here is a half of brick of Ms. Becky, is what I call her, and what you will always call her," Skip explained while holding up half kilo of cocaine in his kitchen to the riveted trio. He walked over to the stove, where he had a pot of boiling water and dumped the cocaine inside, immediately removing the pot to a cold burner, they watched him form the kilo into a kilo and half of rock substance in a matter of minutes artistically. *Damn this nigga giving us the game,* thought D'Shawn. He and Skip got close while doing time in Trenton, New Jersey boot camp for boys at the age of seventeen years old.

Being that East Orange and Newark had their turf differences throughout the years, their relationship as friends was mutual, but distant. When Skip became the man to know, he killed a lot of beef between Newark and East Orange. The trio watched Skip, absorbing every detail of how to cook cocaine and manufacture it into hard rock cocaine.

"I never thought it would be so easy," Lee exclaimed, who was eager to try out their new avenue to getting money by all means to make a profit. *Then, you had to know somebody, and we all knew Skip, who just gave us the game like ABC,* Lee thought.

"I'mma give y'all a half up front to put y'all on, just bring me back my money," Skip said to the trio.

"How much we owe you?" D'Shawn asked.

"I'mma let y'all figure that out on y'alls own, B," Skip retorted.

━━━

"T-Mac let me get $10, I'll pay you back before Christmas," said the lil' eight-year-old who was precocious for his age. His name was Rodney, and the hood's heart was what little Rodney was.

T-Mac knelt down to lil' Rodney's level and asked him sincerely, "Lil' man, you giving me your word, right?"

"Yeah, that's my word, T-Mac, that's all I have as a man!" Rodney retorted, reciting the principle that he'd learned from T-Mac.

"Okay lil' man, then you have $10," T-Mac said, rubbing Rodney on his nappy head, then peeling off ten single one-dollar bills and handing them to Rodney.

"Thank you, T-Mac, you're the best," Rodney said ecstatically, running off to go find his friends in the nearby alley.

T-Mac was the man on 33rd and Santa in Newark, and had mad respect from niggas from all hoods as well. He was twenty-eight years old, and a lookalike of rapper Plies, the ominously grill in T-Mac's mouth was their only distinctiveness. T-Mac was fonder of white gold and had them permanently installed. He was the heroin king, and as well a high-ranking official in the Bloods gang. When he looked down the sidewalk where lil' Rodney had quickly had disappeared, he saw his right-hand man Bean coming up the street with their homie and third in command Chase. Bean and Chase were twenty-eight years old as well, but dark-skinned and stood five-foot-eight, two inches taller than T-Mac. They were all equals, weighing 165lbs solid. The trio had 33rd to 43rd in their pockets, and planned to regulate all of Newark as their clientele increased.

"What's poppin', B?" Exclaimed Bean as he approached T-Mac and pumped his hand vigorously, administering their unique gang shake O.P.

"Five poppin' six droppin' any and every day, Blood," T-Mac retorted.

"What's popping?" T-Mac said Chase pumping T-Mac's hand vigorously as well.

They all were dressed in all-black attire, with red bandanas hanging from their right back pockets, and all of them meticulously carried some type of firearm tucked in their right back pockets. And all of them carried some type of firearm tucked in their waistbands, underneath their t-shirts.

The killing was outrageous in Jersey, East Orange. Neither of the trio was fond of slipping, and was always ready to body a nigga with the quickness and unrelentingly, when it came to turf beef.

"So, what's up with the loud pack?" T-Mac asked Chase, who

had the connect on the best hydro to Dro and Kush that anyone could find.

"Still waiting for the call B. Let's go pick up that work before we get the loud pack," Chase said, knowing that they had heavy duty to take care of, and he preferred to be sober at least halfway through conducting business.

"Okay let's go do that now," T-Mac said.

The trio hopped into T-Mac's conspicuous .745 all-black BMW and prepared to go meet their heroin connect.

CHAPTER 2

WHEN THE FINAL bell resounded at West Orange High, the students, highly elated, rush from the classrooms and out to their cars or buses. This was Varshay's senior year in high school, and she was excited, as well as others in her class, for the Spring Break release.

"No school for two damn weeks!" Varshay exclaimed while walking to her 2016 Optima SX, with desperate pep in her step.

"Yo Varshay! Wait for me, girl!" Her friend since the sandbox named Yalunder yelled out, while slowly walking with her boyfriend Tony P. Yalunder was a high yellow-skinned complexion girl, like Varshay, and one of the top ten beautiful girls after Varshay at West Orange High. She stood five-foot-five, and had a ghetto fabulous booty, most definitely she was the epitome of a coke bottle frame.

"Yo, hurry up. Shit, I got to see my boo, too!" Varshay screamed while jumping inside her Optima that her dad had just painted a pearl white, and had tinted her windows for her.

Her dad worked for a Benz dealership and was slowly ameliorating his status to becoming Vice President soon. Varshay being the most beautiful girl at West Orange High, you would think that the lucky guy would be walking her to her car. But dating schoolmates period was not her cup of tea. Varshay was into street niggas, dope boys, and killers. Something that her dad wasn't approving of, and despite his attempts to control her, his results were feeble as she grew older. His expectations became extraneous because his princess was growing into a gorgeous woman.

Varshay had a boyfriend named T-Mac who gave her large sums of cash at times, and promised her many lies. She was still waiting on her Range Rover that he'd promised her for her seventeenth birthday. As much as she loved him, she was growing tired of the lies. She knew from seeing it herself, and hearing it from her friends, that she wasn't his only girl, something he promised she was. *Niggas are so trifling, but when a bitch fuck on them, it's a problem,* thought Varshay as she waited for her friend Yalunder and Tony P to finish smooching outside the car. She had Monica on a low volume emanating from the Optima's speakers, thinking of what her Spring Break would be like. She had no plans, and both of her parents had to work. She looked at her iPhone 6 and saw that T-Mac still hadn't made effort to call her like she'd told him.

"Hey girl," Yalunder said as she got into the car with her school books from science class.

"Damn, why you looking stressed? I know you ain't tripping on me, 'cause there's plenty of football players where Tony P come from."

"Girl, ain't nobody worrying 'bout these niggas out here. I'm wondering why this nigga ain't calling me yet?" Varshay exclaimed as she navigated out of the school's vicinity.

"So, him not calling got you looking like a mad Diamond?" Said Yalunder frivolously. Being that Varshay favored Lisa Raye, some folks called her Diamond from *Players Club*.

"So, you have jokes," Varshay said, cheering up with a smirk on her face.

"Not really... it's the truth," Yalunder retorted sticking a grape lollipop in her mouth.

"Girl, what are we going to do for Spring Break?" Varshay asked as she came to a red light.

"Tony P and his friends are going to Florida to enjoy the beaches in Miami."

"Fo'real and you not going?" Varshay exclaimed looking at Yalunder. Yalunder pulled the lollipop from her mouth and turned her face up at Varshay in a pout.

"Girl, don't give me that look, that's our Spring Break pass right there. Shit, we ain't got shit else to do," said Varshay.

"Who said he was inviting me or you?" Yalunder asked, pointing at herself then Varshay with the lollipop. "He better, or you better tell him he can't go," said Varshay, proceeding through the green light. "Bitch you know he ain't going to Florida without me or you. Would T-Mac approve of you —"

"Fuck T-Mac! This nigga still ain't calling," said Varshay nonchalantly, frustratingly, and tired of T-Mac's bullshit.

"Well let's go see if he on 33rd."

"Varshay don't chase no nigga, girl you know that," said Varshay.

"I know that's right, girl," Yalunder exclaimed, giving Varshay a high five.

———

"D'Shawn, turn that damn music down I'm tryin' to hear my damn Maury!!" Screamed D'Shawn's mother Connie, with a fat purple haze blunt in her mouth, exhaling the smoke from her mouth and nostrils. D'Shawn was serenading to the Boosie emanating from his speakers he hooked up to his surround system, when he heard his mom Connie screaming over the music.

Damn, I gotta get my own shit and real soon, D'Shawn thought as he turned down the volume to Boosie's new hit, *Welcome Home Boosie.*

"Thank you... Do you want to hit this blunt?"

"Nawl I'm good ma, thank you anyway," D'Shawn retorted.

They were both living in a rowhouse on 121st, along with the roaches and rats. And in the middle of the hood, their rowhouse was adjunct to Lee and Leon's, yet somehow, they were infested with the creatures more than their neighbors. Their grandmother, who lived two rowhouses down, owned the building for more than thirty years. Her name was Ms. Patty Queen, and she was one of them ol'school grannies, who was believed to be sitting on money from the nineties.

Sitting on his king-sized bed, D'Shawn counted all the money that he and his cousins had accumulated from selling the half kilo of cocaine that Skip had given them. Each day, the three of them would head over to 129th and Kentucky to sell dime pieces of rock to the fiends. They took the advice of Skip to sell the entire half in portions of dimes, which the trio saw as prudent and heedful on their end, because the profit was tremendously increasing daily. They were sitting on $40,000 just off of a half, and now contemplating on how much they would give Skip. When he heard the distinctive knocks at his room door, he knew that it was Lee and Leon. For safe measures, he threw back his bed spread over the bundles of money, in case his assumption was disproved. No one, besides the trio, knew that they were hustling, but those on 129th and Kentucky. Once covering up the bundles of money, he hastened over to open his room door.

"What's up cuzzo?" Leon exclaimed with a fat swiss blunt in his hand burning.

"Shit, y'all find a sooner time to come," said D'Shawn closing and locking the door after letting them in.

"So how much do we give Skip?" Asked D'Shawn.

"How much do we got?" Both Leon and Lee said in unison.

"We have forty thousand."

"Forty thousand!" Lee exhilarated,

"Shush! Damn nigga, let the entire hood know our business nigga," Leon exclaimed while D'Shawn shook his head from side-to-side.

"My bad but... Damn, I didn't know we were seeing so much. Is all the product gone?" Lee exclaimed.

D'Shawn walked over to his closet, and retrieved a black Adidas duffel bag, and slowly started transferring the bundles of money inside from the bed. Lee and Leon watched in awe at the pile of money, amazed at how much they'd accumulated as a team.

"I say we give him twenty, and we split twenty amongst ourselves, B," said Leon,

"No, we take twenty and get us a whole brick and do it all over again," said D'Shawn.

The room got quiet momentarily as the trio sat in their contemplative thoughts. All that could be heard was the Boosie playing from the surround system. Lee and Leon on cue both shrugged their shoulders at once. They were all clueless to the prices of a kilo of cocaine, but they were sure that they'd made enough to cop an entire brick.

"That sounds good... let's do it," both brothers said in unison.

Boc! Boc! Boc!

"Ohhh shit!!" Screamed out D'Shawn, hitting the floor with his cousins after hearing the first two shots from the next street that sounded so close by. It was formality that the trio had instinctively been doing for years now. But had never experienced a stray bullet.

Thank God, thought D'Shawn.

When Boo emerged from the back and came into the chatty atmosphere in the visiting lobby, he immediately saw his family gathered at a long table. He hugged his father and mother before he embraced his baby and only sister, and sibling, Varshay.

"Damn sis, you blooming on me," exclaimed Boo as he took in how fast his sister was growing up. *What a fine time to be doing a life sentence when ya little sister is becoming a beach model!* Boo thought regretfully.

"Yeah, she growing up fast," their father spoke.

"I see that," Boo retorted.

"I can't stay little forever," said Varshay, catching on to her dad's sly remark.

Boo wasn't naïve to have missed tension amongst daughter, and overprotective father. It was inevitable that Varshay would come into age. Boo was serving a life sentence in Trenton State Penitentiary for a murder he didn't commit during a convenience store robbery. His codefendant was the gunman who killed the store clerk, but being that the robbery resulted in a homicide, they both were hit with the same murder. Their parents had left to go purchase food for him, and left him and Varshay alone to speak amongst themselves.

"So sis, what's the thug that dad's not approving of?" Asked Boo, getting straight to the point, taking his sister by surprise.

"Yeah I know... so who is he?"

"Dad talk too much."

"Who is he?" Boo said sternly, letting Varshay know that he was serious, and still overprotective of his little sister. He knew that their flawless high yellow complexion was honey for the bees, and his sister was in a world full of lust and not love all alone.

"His name is T-Mac," Varshay said,

"T-Mac from 33rd?" Boo asked drawing back.

"Yeah T-Mac from 33rd," Varshay retorted.

Boo's facial expression revealed that he too wasn't approving of his sister dating a street nigga, but he knew that it was only so much he could do being incarcerated. Plus, his sister was growing older and instead of being rancorous towards her decisions, he decided to give his sister game instead of chastising her.

"Varshay, you too old for me or dad to make your decisions for you and neither of us should be jumping down your throat. But just be careful of who you give your heart to, and know who you are laying down with."

"I'm not having sex, Boo," Varshay said lying through her teeth and realizing that Boo wasn't buying it, evident from the look on his face.

"Tell that one to mom and dad, Varshay. I know who T-Mac is, and he ain't no patient ass nigga either."

"I miss you Boo, I just can't wait until you come home. When you left, T-Mac was the one who started looking out for me. No one else, and I love him," Varshay said on the verge of tears.

"Baby sister, just be safe, okay," Boo said, rubbing Varshay's hand across the table.

"Here comes mom and dad with your food," Varshay said, cheering up. She honestly could say that she respected how her brother accepted her decisions. *To no surprise, every street nigga would,* Varshay thought.

CHAPTER 3

"BITCH BETTER HAVE MY MONEY!"

"Bitch better have my money!"

The crunk crowd serenaded to the lyrics of Rihanna's hit pouring from the massive club's speakers. Club Morosa on 19th and Terrence was full beyond its capacity inside, and still had a mile-long line outside, anticipating on getting inside. Club Morosa was the place to be every Saturday night. Then taking the after party to IHOP restaurant in East Orange, where shit got stupid on occasion. The smart ones avoided the after party and took their ass home, or to a motel with a bad bitch.

"Damn nigga, this joint super swole!" Leon screamed at D'Shawn over the loud music pouring from the massive speakers.

"Hell yeah, nigga. It's hoes everywhere too!" D'Shawn retorted, holding a bottle of coconut Cîroc in his hand. The trio made a fly appearance tonight in their all-black identical Nautica creased outfits with black Timberland boots. Their jewelry was conspicuous and scintillating. It was evident to everyone that knew them, that a change had occurred amongst them. New money, attitude, and power.

"Them niggas look like new money to me," Bean said to T-Mac, who was regulating a dark corner with a bitch named Tracy, who was one of the baddest of bitches thus far in the club. She had an enormous, succulent, firmed ghetto fabulous booty. She had to pull down her mini Yuki dress continually as she threw her ass backwards, ramming into T-Mac's crotch area enticingly. He held onto her gyrating hips dancing to Kelly Rowland's hit *Kisses Down Low*.

"As long as they continue to steal cars for theirs, they okay. We in the dope game, not hotwiring cars homie," T-Mac told Bean, slowly sliding his hands up Tracy's dress, as she grinded seductively on the erection; bulging through his 8732 Young Jeezy jeans. When Tracy felt T-Mac's hard-on and his hand caressing her smooth, stallion caramel thighs and ass, she came up and stood on her tip toes, vibrating both of her ass cheeks in his hands.

"You think that you could handle all this pussy?" Tracy screamed over the music at T-Mac.

"T-Mac got dick fo'days, baby!" T-Mac retorted then slid his fingers between her sweaty ass crack.

"Nah boy! That's exactly where I want it too!!" said Tracy, bending over, poppin' her booty as she got low to the ground.

T-Mac had heard a lot about Tracy and her freaky voracious sex drive. She was originally from Miami, Florida, and decided to move up North for a change of scenery years ago. When she moved to the East Side in Newark, she got with a big-time dope boy from 26th and snake, named Rolex. When Rolex was killed, Tracy moved back to Miami, and got into stripping. Her Roxy Reynolds resemblance got her paid big time. Until another man of hers was robbed, killed, and now she was back in Brick City, where only a few niggas could tell you how great her pussy was. T-Mac planned on joining those statistics after tonight, and if not tonight, then real soon, before she ended up giving it to the entire hood or committing to another dope boy.

"So, what's up with you tonight?" T-Mac said into Tracy's ear, simultaneously sticking his tongue inside her ear seductively. "Come home with me," he retorted.

"I'm with my girl Shenna, I gotta tell her to go home without me first!" Tracy fired back.

"Shenna from 38th and Blackington?" T-Mac asked intrigued.

"'Yeah!" Tracy retorted.

"That's my cousin!" Said T-Mac perplexed, because he knew that his cousin Shenna was a straight lesbian and got mo' pussy than a nigga daily.

"Boy, don't look like that. Shenna my girl, besides I'm strictly dickly!" Tracy exclaimed over a Drake song.

"Okay... Well, do that 'cause we bouncing at 2:00AM!" T-Mac said while looking at his Hublot watch.

"Okay, I'll be back!" Tracy retorted immediately storming off to go find T-Mac's cousin, Shenna, who was smooching on the dance floor with her girlfriend Cyna Red.

"Yo Blood, you 'bout to hit that huh?" Bean asked wasted, but able to control himself, something that T-Mac loved. Let Bean tell it, he was more on point when he was wasted.

"Hell yeah, I'm 'bout to fuck shorty 'til dawn homie!" T-Mac screamed over the speakers, simultaneously pumpin' Bean's hand.

Chase was on the floor getting it down with two chocolate hood hoes named Reese and Erica from 18th and Monterey. They were dressed in almost nothing, identically. For an out of town nigga, they were all game, but not for a Brick City nigga, who knew them as the hood's train.

"Out of all the hoes in this bitch, Chase chose to grind on them dirty pussy ass hoes," Bean said.

"Look at 'em Blood... he drunk," T-Mac said, then erupted in laughter with Bean joining him.

"Yeah that nigga stupid drunk!" said Bean.

Varshay had told her parents that she would be spending the weekend at her friend Yalunder's house in Newark to give them their personal space. In truth, she wanted to be closer to T-Mac, and sad to say, her parents knew it as well. They were love birds at one time, so nothing was new under the sun to them. But neither of her parents were as down to the street mentality as she was. They were Harvard graduates, and raised in suburbs all their lives.

T-Mac had no clue that Varshay was staying over Yalunder's place for the weekend. Yalunder resided in the hood in West Newark. The Crip's turf, prohibiting T-Mac from roaming freely, being that he was a Blood member, and that Yalunder stayed in the area where they actually hung out at, a red flag couldn't go unnoticed in her neighborhood. That didn't stop T-Mac from furtively sliding to pick Varshay up if he had to. They were dressed like twins in a satin Alexander McQueen dress and heels. The dress was tight-fitting and accentuated their delicate curves. They were finally glad to get through the doors at Club Morosa after paying extra because of their ages.

"Eighteen right around the corner, we won't have to be paying to get past go!" Yalunder screamed to Varshay over the loud music.

"Yeah...right!" Varshay retorted.

In their cream dress and heels, heads turned from all directions at their undulations. It was evident to everyone that two gorgeous women had stepped in the place, stealing the show from the decent-looking bitches.

"Girl, do you see him!" Varshay screamed while slapping lustful hands away that molested her ass while moving through the crowded club.

"Nawl, not yet. He probably in one of the VIP sections!" said Yalunder.

They both were on a mission of finding T-Mac and Tony, who had no clue that their main bitches were trying to surprise them. When Varshay looked to the left she saw T-Mac's homeboy Bean getting it on with some skinny girl. When Bean and the girl got low to the ground in their groove, all the breath in her body stopped at once, as she stood in her tracks watching T-Mac kissing on another bitch.

"Bitch, look!" Varshay said grabbing Yalunder by her arm and pointing in T-Mac's direction.

"Dirty ass nigga!" Yalunder screamed, feeling the pain that Varshay had in her chest and stomach.

"Stay strong, girl!" Yalunder said, trying to console her friend.

"How and he's doing it right in front of me!" Cried out Varshay, unable to bridle the tears from falling.

"What do you want to do? We came to have fun, but we could go stump him and that hoe!" Screamed Yalunder, hyped up and ready to get her hood on.

"Nawl, he ain't even worth it and she don't look it, either. Look at that hoe's tits hanging like an old dog's rusty nuts!" Varshay said, cheering up wiping away her tears.

"Ooh shit! Nigga!" Yalunder screamed, startled at the hands clamping onto her booty cheeks like crabs. When she turned around ready to slap whoever's bold ass it was, she saw her man Tony P, and his homeboy Peanut, who had to be the ugliest nigga in the club.

"What you two Aces of Hearts doing in here? Ain't it past y'all's bedtimes?" Tony P screamed over the loud Rich Homie Quan song.

"Then that means it's past yours as well, nigga... you not eighteen yet!" Yalunder said snatching the bottle of Peach Cîroc from Tony P's hand.

"Stop being rude and speak!" Yalunder said, punching Tony P in his chest frolicking some, and admiring his fresh to death outfit.

"What's up Varshay? You look like a Pitbull ready to strike its owner. You okay, Diamond?" Tony P asked while Peanut lustfully eyed Varshay down, abashed to say two words to her.

"Hey, Tony, P, I'm okay. If you get a chance, tell T-Mac I said fuck him!"

"Ouch! No part in that, I knew I saw fire in them eyes!" said Tony P, snatching his bottle from Yalunder, who was gulping it down like it was some Kool-Aid.

"Keep playing, this shit ain't no Kool-Aid!"

"Yo what's up, Tony P," said D'Shawn, walking up clapping hands with Tony P.

"What they do, D'Shawn?" said Tony P and Peanut together.

D'Shawn, I heard that name before, thought Varshay as she studied the handsome man that resembled Tyrese Gibson. *Damn he's cute, and look like he getting money out here too,* Varshay thought.

"So, who is these two beautiful ladies, if I may ask?" said D'Shawn, while staring Varshay down.

Tony P grabbed Yalunder and wrapped her in a warming embrace, claiming his territory.

"This wifey here, and that's —"

"My friend Varshay!" Yalunder yelled out, looking up at Tony P, winking her eye.

Varshay looked from D'Shawn to the corner where T-Mac was, and saw him making his way for the exit with the trash he was dancing with on his arm.

"Yo ma, you looking like your nigga in here. If so, I can under—"

"I don't have no nigga, I was looking for someone why you all concern?" Varshay said, a little feisty.

"Nawl, I'm not concerned if you breaking ya neck looking for another nigga. But I'm concern enough to know who you are, 'cause I never seen you around."

"That's because we from West Orange, do you go out there?" asked Varshay.

"Nawl, but I could find my way," D'Shawn said flirtatiously.

"Ooh girl, I think you done met your match!" Yalunder exclaimed.

"Girl, shut up!" Varshay exclaimed, blushing.

"Let's share a bottle and get to know each other, and no, I'm not trying to seduce you for any sex on the first night. You look more appreciative than 90% of the club, and 10% belongs to ya homegirl," D'Shawn said in his smoothest mack game.

Damn, this nigga smooth and sexy as hell. What do he know about appreciation? Varshay thought mesmerized in his handsomeness.

"Okay!" Varshay said before thinking twice.

D'Shawn offered his arm, and she intertwined, taking in the redolence of his Polo cologne.

"Don't get lost or too loose!" said Yalunder, grabbing Varshay's ass.

"Tony P get your wife before I dig in her ass!" Varshay exclaimed, swiping away Yalunder's hand as she walked off with Mr. Handsome Guy. As they undulated through the crowd, D'Shawn winked his eye at Lee and Leon, winning the bet of snatching up the bad chick on his arm. Varshay quickly took notice that no one tried to molest her like before.

Who is this nigga? Whoever he is, these niggas respect him, thought Varshay. Neither her nor D'Shawn took notice of Bean mugging them and snapping pictures of them with his iPhone 6.

CHAPTER 4

WHEN T-MAC WOKE up to the smell of eggs and the sound of sizzling bacon, he was hit with an overwhelming feeling of nausea from all of the liquor that he'd surfeit last night. He quickly jumped up from bed and hastened over to the master bedroom's bathroom. Once inside, he instantly embraced the toilet and vomited all the liquor in his stomach. When he was done, he wiped his mouth with the back of his hand. When he felt the perspiration on his face, he stripped down to nothing and hopped in the shower. As the steaming hot water cascaded his body, it brought life to him energetically. He felt like a totally different, rejuvenated person. A smile swept across his face when he thought about how his night had turned out. The moment that him and Tracy made it to his suite in Englewood Palace on his 113th in South Newark, they explored each other's bodies from the living room to the bedroom.

I gave that hoe the business! T-Mac loftily, thought to himself while rubbing his morning erection. *That bitch got some good pussy, I gotta put her on speed dial,* he thought as he emerged from the shower. T-Mac quickly dried himself, then finished his hygiene. When he walked into the kitchen in his Polo briefs and white wife beater, he caught a splendid sight of Tracy at the stove wearing nothing but a black satin thong and a matching bra. She had one hand on her hip and the other stirring a spoon in a pot of grits.

"Damn!" T-Mac mumbled as he walked up to Tracy and rubbed her ass and thighs romantically, while looking over her shoulders.

"What you call this, appreciation from how good I took care of you last night ma?" T-Mac asked.

"No, I actually call this a woman's duty. I have other ways to show my appreciation for a good performance. Don't act like you did all the work now," said Tracy as she moved over to grab two slices of wheat bread. The way her succulent ass jiggled made T-Mac want to halt her and fuck her right where she stood.

"So, you never had a woman cook breakfast for you?" Tracy asked, throwing a slab of butter in the frying pan.

Not in my own shit, T-Mac wanted to say badly.

"Only a couple times," T-Mac said, not wanting to sound lame.

"Only a couple, huh?" Tracy retorted, nonchalantly.

"What, you don't believe me?" T-Mac asked.

"Nawl, I could only take a man's word," Tracy said, turning off the heat to all the pots on the stove.

When she turned around and looked T-Mac in his eyes, he took in the sight of how beautiful Tracy actually was, without her heels on she stood five-foot-five and with no second looks, resembled the model Roxy Reynolds from head to toe in all areas. She wrapped her arms around his waist and stood and nibbled on his exposing nipple that peeked from his wife beater.

"So, this is how you show your appreciation?" T-Mac asked, while caressing Tracy's smooth ass.

"Nope!" Tracy responded, quickly immersing down low and grabbing a hold of T-Mac's erected dick.

Tracy slowly stroked his dick before placing him in her mouth at mid-length of his eight inches. As she slowly sucked his dick passionately, T-Mac held on to the back of her head, enjoying the ecstasy of her fellation.

"Damn ma!" T-Mac purred as he began to fuck Tracy's mouth. After five minutes, he was cumming.

"Umm! Umm!" Tracy moaned out, simultaneously keeping pace with the rhythm to T-Mac's thrusts.

"Damn baby, I'm cumming! Arghhh!" T-Mac groaned out, releasing his load in Tracy's mouth, who swallowed every drop, seductively.

"Damn ma, I gotta keep you around," T-Mac breathlessly exclaimed.

"Be careful what you requesting. I may be too much for you. Plus, you have a girlfriend, don't act like I don't know," Tracy exclaimed.

While T-Mac slept, Tracy had a conversation with her girl Shenna, and she'd given her the 411 on T-Mac's woman problem, and informed her 'bout his young wifey.

"So, what that mean?" T-Mac asked perplexed.

"It means just because you got it on the first night, don't mean it's all ice cream and candy. I'll be around, but don't put no stipulations on what you can't handle," said Tracy, while fixing T-Mac a fat plate of cheese grits, eggs, bacon, blueberry muffins, and ham.

Damn, I may have underestimated this bitch. She may give me a run for my money, and Varshay... hell nawl, Varshay the baddest bitch that hit the Jersey area, and the only dick she's getting is from me! T-Mac thought.

"Here, sit down and eat, and give yourself time to think. No need to rush nothing, I enjoyed myself," Tracy said, handing T-Mac his plate and tapping his sensitive penis. He watched her walk out the kitchen. "I'm about to take a shower, then I have to bounce. Will you take me to Shenna?" Tracy asked over her shoulder.

"Acourse boo!" T-Mac responded with a mouth full of food. *Damn this bitch can cook!* He thought as he ate the delicious breakfast.

Despite her having a tremendously great time last night with D'Shawn, evident from her hangover, it wasn't enough to assuage the pain that she was experiencing after seeing T-Mac with the trashy hoe. *I can't believe him,* Varshay thought as tears cascaded down her face. She wiped her face with her shirt as she scrolled through the channels absentmindedly on Yalunder's living room flat screen TV. She'd slept in bed with Yalunder until she heard Yalunder's mother Ms. Lulu stick her head in and announced that she and Yalunder's little brother Travis were off to Church.

When Varshay heard the silence linger after their departure, she realized that sleep had gone a far distance. She arose from Yalunder's queen sized bed, and confided in peace in her family living room. The TV was on mute, and she'd been crying from the moment she sat down on the plush white leather sofa with her feed tucked under her. She hated T-Mac and realized that she was ready to move on from him. *Maybe it's time for me to try new things,* she thought. It was hard for her to finalize, because T-Mac had been the only man she'd had sex with, after he broke her cherry at sixteen years old.

That's all it was to him...sex, because he didn't love me. If he did, he wouldn't be disrespecting me the way he did...fuck T-Mac! Varshay thought angrily, as Yalunder walked into the living room in her pink Betty Boop boy shorts and white sports bra.

"Hey girl, why you in here with the TV on mute?" Yalunder asked, flopping down on the sofa next to Varshay. *Damn she's hurt!* Yalunder thought seeing Varshay's red eyes from crying.

"Just had to get some peace girl. As much fun as I had last night, I still can't get over T-Mac's dirty ass," Varshay exclaimed, unable to stop the tears.

"It's okay Varshay, let it out, and decide what you're going to do. I mean, straight up girl, you can't continue to let him do you like this."

"I know... It hurts so much!" Varshay cried out hysterically in her friend's consoling arms. Yalunder hated seeing her friend break down about a no-good ass nigga who only wanted to use her as a souvenir.

"So, what are you going to do? Just because he popped that cherry don't mean y'all is married. It's evident that he showed you that last night," Yalunder said fondling the curls in Varshay's head.

"I'mma leave his ass!" Varshay said sniffling, slowly coming back.

"Good, 'cause I want to see this!" Yalunder exclaimed, jumping from the sofa to go grab Varshay's iPhone 6. When she returned, they called T-Mac's phone twice on speakerphone. Both times getting sent directly to his voicemail.

"He'll come to reality real soon. I'm changing my number today and straight deleting him from my phone contacts, simple as that," Varshay said, drying her face with her t-shirt.

"Simple as that," Yalunder retorted.

The last tears that I will shed for him, thought Varshay as she continued to dry her face.

Bean was always in the trap early to situate all of their daily product. He'd called T-Mac's ass all morning, not getting any answer. So, he was elated to hear T-Mac's distinctive loud car system playing Rich Homie Quan's *Blah, Blah, Blah!* After hearing the system die, Bean prepared to deliver T-Mac the devastating news of his perfidious woman. When he heard the keys turning in the door, he had already pulled up the shocking images from last night of D'Shawn and Varshay together like a happy couple.

"What's poppin', Blood?" T-Mac said, coming through the door dressed in all back with his brim low.

"East Side all day, Blood," Bean retorted, pumping T-Mac's hand vigorously, throwing a "B" up high in the air, then dropping a "C" to the ground.

"Man, that bitch Tracy got some killer pussy, B!" T-Mac exclaimed elated.

"Yeah?"

"Hell yeah B, I'mma have her on my team, nigga. You already know," said T-Mac, walking into the kitchen to fix him a glass of Hennessy.

"Yo, I think you got more to worry about than adding bitches to yo' list, Blood," Bean said straightforwardly.

"Black ass nigga, what's 50?" T-Mac asked, waiting to hear what problems he had to worry about. "If a nigga playing with that money, we bed them, B. Since when have that been a problem," Asked T-Mac

"Man, if a nigga playing with that money, then nigga you wouldn't know until I wash his ass. But when a nigga playing with yo' bitch, I see how you react first."

"Wait a minute... Who's playing with my bitch?" T-Mac asked, seriously concerned, and fully alerted.

"See for yourself," Bean said tossing his iPhone 6 in the air. Swiftly, T-Mac caught the phone and looked at the picture that sent his heart to the ground.

"That's that nigga D'Shawn!" Exclaimed T-Mac.

"Yeah that's him, I told you them niggas look like new money. I heard from Jo Jo that they slanging Ms. Becky hard on 129th and Kentucky."

"Man, this nigga had my bitch in the club with me. No wonder this hoe ain't picking up!" Screamed T-Mac, snatching his black snapback hat from his head and rubbing the pain and frustration from his face into his hands. "Ain't he damu?" Asked T-Mac.

"Nawl, but he food if it's beef," Bean retorted.

CHAPTER 5

D'SHAWN: *So why you not going to MIA with your friend?*

Varshay: *I told you I'm okay I'm just not feeling it, too much on my mind*

D'Shawn: *Too much of me on your mind?*

D'Shawn sat in the barber chair waiting for Mr. Miley to finish with his last customer while texting Varshay. When the text came back, he smiled bright. He was feeling this girl like no other, and wanted to take it slow with her. He knew wifey material when he saw it.

Varshay: *Acourse I'm full of you on my mind... Don't get big headed* 😊 *xo*

D'Shawn: *Practice what you preach beautiful* 😊

Varshay: *Whatever boy lol* 😊 *xo*

"So, what we doing here today, son? The same as usual, or you got something else in mind?" Asked Mr. Miley, who'd been cutting D'Shawn's hair since a youngin, as he wrapped a black barber apron around D'Shawn's neck.

"Just give me a fresh fade, Mr. Miley," said D'Shawn, getting comfortable in the plush barber chair.

He looked at his phone again before closing his eyes. *Let her sweat,* he thought. His boy Tony P, who looked in every aspect like Master P, had invited him to come along with him and his crew to South Florida Beach in Miami, but he declined. He didn't want to leave Lee and Leon by themselves, though they could handle their own. But it was also money to be made. Instead of a brief vacation, D'Shawn was slowly becoming a threat to a lot of niggas in Newark, and it would be too late before any of them had the slightest clue. Skip was showing love every time it was re-up.

As the clippers hit his head, he thought about Varshay and how beautiful she was. She was honest with him about T-Mac, and had told him truthfully that she was over him, and moving on without looking back. D'Shawn wasn't naïve to know you couldn't speak for love alone, it was the actions that made a break-up final. D'Shawn knew of T-Mac and his reputation in the streets. The only difference between him and T-Mac was that T-Mac hand an innumerable body count, to only a few that D'Shawn had. D'Shawn's street cred came from his fierce reputation in fighting. He had a set of hands on him like Mayweather Jr, swift and undefeated. Many people wanted to become his manager and promote him in the ring, but the riveting streets is where his passion was. Stealing cars was his biggest break-through to seeing abundance in cash. Now, he was on to another level in abundance. Next week, he would have cash enough to get him and his two cousins their own wheels. They had money now, but they were still in the building stages. *Soon my nigga, we'll have the entire Newark on lock down,* D'Shawn thought. He felt his iPhone vibrate in his hand, indicating a call coming in. When he looked at the caller, he saw that it was someone important.

"Wait a minute, Mr. Miley. I have to take this call.

"Go ahead, soldier," Mr. Miley responded, cutting the clippers off.

"Yo what's up, B?" D'Shawn answered.

"I need y'all to come pick up three of Ms. Beckys... This one on me, you know the rest," Skip said, business-like.

"How soon?" D'Shawn asked, calm and collect not wanting to

reveal how elated he was. Skip was his nigga, the only nigga that saw his potential, and gave him a chance. So, he would always have Skip's back no matter what. D'Shawn and his crew were too clueless to see that they were paying too much for a key of cocaine. Mr. Miley could've told them so, if he had any clue. The immensity of the cash flowing in was what they'd never had in their life. What they were getting from the Arab stealing cars was nowhere near to what they were getting from the dope game, even though they were being ripped off, unbeknownst to them all.

"Come see me in three hours on 151st and Spruce," said Skip.

━━

T-Mac had tried contacting Varshay and confronting her ass about D'Shawn, but saw that she'd changed her number on him. He was stupefied by her actions.

I can't believe this bitch just stunted on me and have no explanation, T-Mac thought angrily. Trying to reach her on Facebook was exhausting. He had an innumerable count of messages in her inbox, and even tried inboxing her best friend Yalunder's fine ass. She too had no rap for him. When he found out that it was Tony P who'd hooked D'Shawn up with his bitch, T-Mac became fiery at the prospect of how long they'd probably been fucking around on the down low. He hadn't had a chance to step to D'Shawn yet. Truthfully, he didn't want to step down to no nigga about a bitch, but hearing D'Shawn's name ring in the dope game, that seemed a more suitable approach. *I'll ask for a front and don't pay the chump ass nigga back. A real nigga would never war, and that's exactly what I want,* T-Mac thought grimy towards D'Shawn while sitting at a table in his stash house counting stacks of money that came from heroin alone. Bean and Chase were out collecting all the money from traps. Looking at his phone on the table he grabbed it and logged in on Facebook. He pulled up Varshay's page for the umpteenth time and like every when he checked, he saw her relationship status single! Though it read single, it assuaged him a little, because it showed him that her and D'Shawn weren't serious yet. *As long as she stayed serious about being single, I'll always be able to get her back. I popped that cherry, that will always be my pussy,* T-Mac thought as he entered Varshay's inbox and left her another message. When he was done he did the same to Yalunder's inbox.

T-Mac: *Yo your girl trippin, get her to call me ASAP!*

———

Skip was sitting in his conspicuous Range Rover in front of the gambling house when D'Shawn and Lee pulled up in an all-white Ford Focus, that had legal dark tents on all windows. Both of them stepped out of the car, and hopped in with Skip. D'Shawn took the passenger, while Lee climbed into the back seat. The atmosphere was foggy from the purple haze smoke lingering in the air. Skip's normal price on a kilo of cocaine was 18.5 thousand dollars, but he was selling a key faithfully to the ingenious trio for thirty-five thousand a piece. Being that they were selling the kilo in dime piece rocks, and not any tray weight. They were able to see more money, than the actual lost they were taking. Due to Skip's manipulative monopolization. It was money that had been their dream, and they were making Skip's pockets extremely heftier than what he'd imagine would ever happen. When he put them down, his intentions on good business were good, but his grimy deal of getting over on the trio seemed more dulcet.

"Listen, I'mma give y'all what y'all came for, and front y'all three on that. Just bring me twenty-five for each one I front."

Damn, he going down on the price, we slowly becoming his A team, thought D'Shawn.

"So, twenty-five instead of thirty-five, correct?" Asked D'Shawn, for assurance of the stipulations.

"Just this one time," Skip retorted, putting one finger up. "And that's because I want to see y'all double up on this round. Remember dime it to the last dime, even if you have to cut a nickel rock. Sell it," Skip stipulated with so much enthusiasm that it motivated D'Shawn and Lee to trap hard for that cash.

As long as they sold kilos by the drudgery dime, they'd never know what a loss was, Skip thought impishly. "When y'all put this through, I'mma introduce y'all to a bad boy in the game. I call him Cyna man or simply, that boy," said Skip.

"Deal," D'Shawn exclaimed, ready for whatever and speaking for all. After they conducted business and were gone, Skip walked into the gambling house a richer man than yesterday. His ol'school friends were waiting on his arrival.

<hr>

"Girl, I really hate that you're letting me go to Miami alone."

"I know, but what am I supposed to do while you and Tony P cozy up and get y'alls freak on?" Varshay said to Yalunder, who was laying 'cross her bed.

Varshay's parents were at work, so her and Yalunder had the place to themselves. For hours now, Yalunder had been in a piteous adamant mood, trying to get Varshay to come along with her to Miami. But tenaciously, her friend had her mind made up. After asking D'Shawn did he want to come along and getting his declination. Her spirits of going to the sunny beaches in her sexy bikini quickly became dull and vanished.

"Girl, just take pictures and FaceTime me, it'll be just as if I was there with you," Varshay said, then flopped down on the bed next to Yalunder.

"I guess," Yalunder exclaimed, releasing a yielding sigh.

Varshay's mind was on D'Shawn and getting to know him and everything about him. She was digging his entire swagger, and most of all his patience of not rushing things. *He seems different from them all,* Varshay thought to herself.

"Girl, what are you going to do about T-Mac all in my damn inbox?" Yalunder exclaimed, irksomely.

"Child, I don't see why he ain't getting the picture," Varshay said nonchalantly They both were in their iPhones logged in on Facebook, strolling through the newsfeed, and checking their inboxes, T-Mac had 150 messages in each of their inboxes, and they both were tired. Finally, Varshay had enough of seeing him beg for her back.

"Girl, watch this," said Varshay, with a pout as she prepared to write a post on Facebook.

Varshay Diamond: *When niggas have it good, why don't they realize it until... It's gone?*

Varshay posted her message on Facebook, immediately getting fifty likes in under two minutes.

"I know that's right, girl!!" screamed out Yalunder ecstatically.

She was happy to see that her friend had found a new boo thang, and had ditched that no-good ass nigga T-Mac. *I just hope that she don't be like most of us women and go back to the man that had done us wrong,* thought Yalunder.

CHAPTER 6

"Go baby, run! Run! Run! Run!" Yalunder and Varshay shouted out ecstatically from the home bleachers as they watched Tony P scramble out of the pocket, past the lunge of scrimmage in a turbo blast, and dive into the end zone for a touchdown. Increasing the ridiculous score to 27-0.

"Girl, that boy is serious!" Shouted Varshay excited to see Tony P's amazing performance as a West Orange High quarterback. Beside her, recording the game to place it on YouTube, was D'Shawn.

"D'Shawn did you get it, baby?" Varshay shouted, throwing her arm around his neck as he sat down on the metal bleacher to review the play that had the home team fans in exhilaration.

"You know we got to YouTube this shit, that nigga goin' pro!" D'Shawn screamed over the ovation in the football stadium.

"You got that right, D'Shawn. My boo going pro!" Yalunder cheered on.

Varshay stood and gave Yalunder high five, and continued to watch the game after the extra point showed good, bringing the score to 28-0. Varshay and Yalunder both dressed like twins in a pink custom-made jersey with Tony P's name and jersey #1 in white embellished, glittered laid letters. The white PZI jeans they wore accentuated their nicely curvaceous, ghetto fabulous asses. They straight killed the dress code with the pink suede Timberland boots, and had envious females everywhere. They were the two most gorgeous bitches at Tall Head Stadium. And until Tony P made it off the field, they both belonged to D'Shawn. *I wish that I could fuck both of them at the same time... only if Tony P wasn't my dawg, I'd try my luck. I see how that bitch be eating up on the low... Or is that an illusion?* Thought D'Shawn mesmerized, as he looked at both of the beautiful women in his presence.

Varshay looked back at D'Shawn if she could feel him burning holes in her jeans. He was fortunate to be caught staring at her ass... and not her friend's. Their eyes locked for a couple seconds, before Varshay gave in and gave a giddy smile, blushing like never before. When she turned around and got back in the game, D'Shawn prided himself bigtime.

I know she fucked up about the boy! He thought confidently, as he resumed back recording the game. Tony P was the best thing coming out of Jersey, period. He was like Cam Newton in all aspects. At six-foot-five and weighing 220lbs, he was dominating every high school in the district. And was now about to win West Orange High it's first state title championship against Norman High, a team that's been undefeated for the last ten years!

D'Shawn watched as Tony P scrambled left out of the pocket and sent a Hail Mary down left field to wide receiver, Tory Gray, who was another Larry Fitzgerald. When Tory caught the forty-eight-yard bomb and pedaled backwards into the end zone for another touchdown, the stadium went berserk!

The score was now 34-0, a complete blow out and embarrassment.

"Oh my gosh!" Yalunder exclaimed, covering her mouth in deep astonishment. *This man is the truth, and a meal ticket out of poverty, Lord!* She thought as tears came in a flood down her red, cheerful face.

"D'Shawn, did you get that!" Shouted Varshay over the stadium's ovation, looking back at D'Shawn, who nodded his head up and down in an affirmative gesture as, yes. When she looked back and saw the tears falling from her friend's eyes, she immediately embraced Yalunder.

"Girl, why you crying? Them better be tears of joy!" Varshay shouted, already being accustomed to her friend's surge of emotions whenever she saw Tony P defeat a team.

"That man is amazing!" Yalunder said, drying her eyes with her t-shirt underneath her jersey.

"Girl he's going pro, you better believe that!" Said Varshay still holding onto Yalunder, as they both watched the extra point bam through successfully, bringing the score to a shameful 35-0.

"Girl, I'm okay... you know I get emotional watching this man play... go see about your man."

"My man!?" Varshay exclaimed looking at Yalunder like she was crazy.

"You heard me, because that's the only nigga you want to talk about... don't make me blast your ass!" Said Yalunder.

"You got that, bitch!" Varshay retorted then sat down next to D'Shawn and intertwined her arms through his one arm. She enjoyed his comfort, smell, conversation that lasted to the wee hours in the morning, and his elegance, most definitely. He was fresh in his all-black Gucci sweat suit advertising nothing but a big money sign with his iced-out chain and other conspicuous jewelry on his wrist and fingers. The wad accentuating from his pockets was hefty and D'Shawn made Varshay's availability to it known that she was welcome to every last dollar in his pocket, if she so desired. It's been two weeks since Spring Break ended and D'Shawn still hadn't pressured her for any sex. Bad as she wanted him to fuck her into exhaustion, she respected his respect for her as a young woman. His perspectives of how he saw her meant a lot to her because no man had ever treated her so appreciative and queenly in the manner D'Shawn did. Not even T-Mac, who broke my fucking virginity. *Just to be in some virgin pussy, he never loved me,* thought Varshay.

"What's on your mind, beautiful?" D'Shawn asked Varshay, bringing her mind back to earth.

"You," Varshay exclaimed mirthfully while looking into his eyes with lust.

"C'mere ma," D'Shawn said leaning into her, placing his lips to hers gently. She opened her mouth and allowed him to slide his tongue inside. Passionately and slow, he kissed her, sending an electrifying climax throughout her body.

"Umm," Varshay managed to let out a soft moan as D'Shawn sucked on her bottom lip, passionately. He pecked her two times before he stopped then stared in her gorgeous eyes. The cozy duo was experiencing something ineffable and anticipating what didn't need to be explained for neither.

"Just don't hurt me, D'Shawn," Varshay said teary-eyed. Before the tears could fall from the wells of her eyes, D'Shawn wiped them away.

"Can I hold you to them same stipulations?' he asked Varshay looking her in her eyes.

"Yes, D'Shawn, you could hold me to the same," Varshay retorted, cracking on emotions. This time it was Varshay initiating the deeply passionate kiss.

"Awww!!" Exclaimed Yalunder as she looked back at the two new lovers.

"Girl shut up, and get some business!" Shouted Varshay.

Her classmates saw her new man, people she'd never seen in her life, and the envious cheerleaders who wanted the contentedness that she now had. But no one saw the fire burning in T-Mac's eyes who was watching the couple in the upper crown with enough fire in his eyes to torch the entire stadium.

CHAPTER 7

BEAN HAD INCONSPICUOUSLY EMERGED from the black SS Impala on 56th and Drake and in a hastened strut. He took an alley, heading towards 57th and Charleston. Dressed in an all-black, hoodie sweater, gloves, and jeans, he was able to blend in with the midnight darkness well. The close sounds of furious dogs barking could be heard. He knew they were barking off of instinct and could smell the danger approaching its prey. It was East Newark, Brick City, and the dogs too lived in a high crime neighborhood. Every step of the way Bean took with precaution. Someone could easily stick their head out a side window to the closed section of the rowhouses and turn his day red. But only those who was aware of his coming would accomplish anything close to it, and only one individual was aware. When he came to the end of the alley, he meticulously surveyed his surroundings. It was dead, just liked he'd been informed. When he emerged from the alley he made a sharp right, and walked three rowhouses down until he came upon a crew of junkies standing outside; lingering on the abandoned rowhouse steps. When they say Bean, everyone but one tensed up. The individual that was expecting Bean was amongst the junkies, fearless.

"Where is he?" Bean spoke with nefarious look in his impish eyes.

The individual looked at Bean and furtively nodded his head towards the entrance of the abandoned rowhouse, and that's all Bean needed to know. When he walked up to the filthy stairs, and entered the rowhouse, all the junkies slowly made an exit. Bean stood in the living room of the roach and rat infested, out of order rowhouse that was listed as abandoned from the poor condition. It was being used for a brothel amongst the junkies, as well a crack house.

The smell of crack, urine, and feces redolently lingered in the air as Bean made his way towards the intensified sounds of a woman moaning. When Bean made it to the room where the moans came louder, he pulled underneath his sweater, and grabbed his Glock .50. In one smooth motion, Bean centered himself in the doorway, and got a view of the illuminated room from a cheap single lit candle. He saw on a floor mattress, a junkie named Sarah Lee getting fucked from the back, doggy style aggressively, by a big black muscular dude who had no clue that Bean was in the picture, front row seat. But Sarah Lee did. Her eyes grew wide in fear when she saw the Glock .50 in Bean's hand.

"Frey! Frey! Nooo! Pleaseee!!" Sarah Lee screamed out in panic trying her best to scramble away from the approaching danger. But unfortunately, she was unable to escape Frey's firm death grip on her hips. It was obvious that Frey mistook her sudden panic as trying to run away from his rapid penetration, because he intensified his thrusting, trying to damage the good pussy that he'd paid for.

"Bitch, stop running and take this dick!" Frey shouted out in lustful rage.

"No Frey! Nooo!"

Bean aimed at Sarah Lee's face that had nowhere to run, looking back at him crammed against the base of the floor and the dirty mattress ass up, face down, and pulled the trigger.

BOOM! BOOM!

"What the fuck!" Frey shouted coming out of the good pussy as

Sarah Lee's head exploded in a splatter of blood and brains onto the wall, mattress, and his groin area. When Frey saw Bean, he backed into a corner with his hands up, still erected.

"Hey man, what's up?" Frey asked timorously, trembling in surrender.

"Where my money, Frey?" Bean asked with the Glock aimed at Frey's chest.

"Man, I... I... Got to—"

"Wrong answer Frey, we put you on, and this how you repay us by tricking off with these junkies. That's what you think we are, huh? You smoking again, and what we told you Frey, 'bout smoking."

"Man, it's alright. I got—"

"Shut the fuck up nigga, it's bed time!"

BOOM!

"Ahhh!" Frey screamed at the top of his lungs as the bullet hit him in his groin area. As Frey slouched over in pain, Bean hit him in his face three times, taking all lights out.

BOOM! BOOM! BOOM!

Skip had just hit the poker game for $1500, leaving his ol'school contenders with another failed shot at takin' his title. *I don't know why they continue to let me play,* Skip thought as he sat in his Range Rover outside the gambling house, getting his dicked sucked by Monique. *One thing about this fast ass bitch is that she can suck a dick like super head,* Skip thought. Watching how skillful she was amazed him. With his seat reclined back, and smoking on a phat purple haze swiss blunt, he felt like a king. Her slurping sound effects was music to his ears.

"So, where Trina with that fat ass booty of hers?" Skip asked Monique inquiring 'bout her girlfriend. Monique made a loud slurping sound as she came up to answer Skip.

"Trina at home, why? Do you want me to call her, too?" Monique licked the tip of Skip's dick then downed his enormous length to his balls, simultaneously stroking him perfectly.

"Do you want me to, huh?" Monique asked. Skip looked at Monique with lust-filled eyes. She was a curvaceous bitch and had a killer body. *The bitch just loves them damn black stank ass booty shorts, but the pussy is good,* Skip thought.

"Nawl, put that dick back in ya mouth I'll catch her on another round," said Skip.

"Okay," Monique said then resumed back to sucking Skip's dick. He'd been fucking Monique and Trina since he could remember, when they both were fifteen years old, pussy first in the streets. The entire East Side of East Orange knew what their roast beef pussies looked like, and tasted like. *Niggas had to be a fool to eat these hoes' pussy,* Skip thought. He felt himself cumming and closed his eyes, enjoying the pleasurable climax.

"Yesss Lord, yesss girl," Skip exclaimed in ecstasy as he released his load in Monique's mouth. When Monique had swallowed every seed that discharged, she fixed her rusty ass weave and tossed out her hand; palm open.

"Money time," Monique exclaimed. *This bitch 'bout her money fo' real,* Skip thought as he peeled off two hundred dollars from his phat wad, and placed it in Monique's hand. The smile on her face looked as if she'd just experienced her first happy meal.

"Thank you, Skip," Monique said, stuffing the money in her bra.

"I'll see you later, Monique," Skip said nonchalantly, unlocking the door for Monique to get out his shit. Monique looked at Skip like he was stupid.

"Skip, you not goin' to take me home? it's too damn dark out there, and I don't even live 'round here," Monique purred sadly.

"So, what the fuck you think Money would get you at?" Skip said.

"Robbed, 'cause I ain't from 'round here, nigga," Monique retorted, with an impish pout on her face.

"Bitch get out my shit, you and Trina slang more pussy than I gets on a regular, ain't nobody worried 'bout yo' ass," Skip said, already knowing that Monique only wanted to be seen stepping out his shit so that she'd have something to brag about.

"Man, fo'real," Monique purred.

"And I ain't goin' to tell you again, fo'real," Skip said.

When Monique saw the look on his face, she sucked her teeth, then made her exit. He watched her walk off the block in a hasten, before he started his Range Rover and left the area himself. He had the streets on lock in East Orange and soon he would make a man in Newark regulate to his perspectives. He had the right nigga, who had no clue what laid beyond selling a ten-dollar rocks of cocaine, and what buying a kilo for 18.5 was. He wished that he could manipulate a lot of niggas in the dope game like D'Shawn and his cousins, but unfortunately, a lot of niggas in the streets knew the real fundamentals. So, the approach would be vain, and could trigger war. Skip was ready to introduce D'Shawn to the heroin game. *If I get him to take over the heroin game, and leave him dumb to the cocaine game, there wouldn't be any skepticism on his behalf. Just as long as he kept the cocaine going dime for dime, nothing more nothing less. I'll have the game circled in a year fucking with ducks,* Skip thought to himself, masterminding and setting his ducks in place.

The game is to win and if cheating get you to win, then it's all part of the game too, Skip thought as he blasted his Rick Ross hit.

"Every day em hustling, every day, every day, every day em hustling!" Skip serenaded the lyrics of Rick Ross blaring from his thunderous surround system.

"Em that nigga, B, motherfuckin' Skip!" Skip shouted out feeling himself and his new scheme against his rival friend D'Shawn.

"Damn, I wish my mama and daddy could see me today," Skip said of his dead parents and only family he knew after moving from Florida years ago. His parents were the ones who taught him the masters of the dope game. The same game that cost them their lives, was yearning to end Skip's as well. But he was too greedy and grimy to see the predestined shadows of death.

CHAPTER 8

THE THREE BLACK luxurious .745 BMW's pulled off the dealership lot in a follow the leader parade. They were on their way to the rim shop now to purchase a nice set of 22" rims. D'Shawn led the pack through traffic, not caring about the jakes, because him and his cousins now were legit drivers, obtaining a Jersey driver's license. *The dope game is way too sweet,* D'Shawn thought. He couldn't wait to show off his new baby to the niggas in the hood. Him and his cousins had stacked their paper, now it was time for them to look like some real money.

D'Shawn turned into Bobby's Rims, also known as the chop shop, where it all started for the trio. Lee parked behind D'Shawn and Leon behind Lee.

"Damn, who Rover is that!?" Leon asked, pointing at a conspicuous pink Range Rover on 28" Forgiatos.

"I don't know. But if it's a he, that nigga must be sweet, straight up, and they from Camden... At least that's what the plates say," Lee said.

Then they saw the beautiful coke bottle framed woman walking towards the Rover, in some skin tight PZE jeans accentuating her enormous ass booty. She was gorgeous and resembled the model Blac Chyna from head to toe.

"Damn D'Shawn, that shorty got back, B," said Leon.

"Yeah. More than you could handle, nigga," D'Shawn retorted.

"Man watch this, I bet I get the number," Leon said confidently

"Oh yeah... Two hundred that you don't," D'Shawn challenged, pulling off two hundred dollars from his phat wad.

"Give me the money," Lee said, holding out his hand to collect.

"Alright," said Leon producing his half.

D'Shawn and Leon both put their money in Lee's hand.

"Go fat boy, let me see you pull shorty," D'Shawn said.

"Nigga watch and learn," Leon said, then strutted off towards the pink Range Rover.

"Let's see if Arab goin' to let us get a '," Lee said ready to upgrade his whip already.

Him and D'Shawn walked into the shop while Leon hung inside the driver window of the Range Rover.

"Whoever her nigga is, he got some coke. I be hearing how them Camden niggas be eating, that's heroin city," D'Shawn exclaimed.

"Maybe she got a bitch," Lee retorted.

"Then that mean Leon ain't got no win," D'Shawn exclaimed laughing.

Once inside, Lee called for Bobby personally. He was the first one who started working for Bobby. So, it was him who always dealt with Bobby when it came to business. The sexy brunette walked toward the back to go get Bobby. D'Shawn and Lee couldn't help but stare at all her ass eatin' away her black booty shorts.

"Bobby keep him some bad bitches on the clock," said Lee. D'Shawn turned around and put his back up against the counter to check up on Leon, and his mac game. When he saw Leon smiling from the back window partially let down on the Rover, he knew that he'd lost the bet against Leon.

"Fat boy pearly whites always got them hoes out their drawls," D'Shawn said.

"And the way he ate their asses," Lee threw in. D'Shawn wasn't surprised to see Leon pulling a bad bitch. The women were fucked up about Leo. His risibility of getting a good laugh was hilarious. And his last name alone held an enormous quantity of weight.

"Hello, my main man Lee, what brings?" Bobby said in his Arabic accent, grabbing Lee and D'Shawn's attention.

"Like always, business Bobby, but not the usual," said Lee letting Bobby know that this wasn't no chop shop business.

"Come will you. I've been waiting to see you personally. Let's converse in my office," said Bobby waving Lee back.

"Wherever I go, my cousin comes, Bobby. Talkin' to me like talkin' to him as well," Lee said to Bobby who waved understanding, nonchalantly.

"I understand, he's welcome too. Come now, both of you," said Bobby leading the way down a short hallway behind the counter, and to an opulent spacious office.

Everything in the office epitomized Arab money. Bobby had white immaculate bear fur laid on the floor of the cocaine plush carpet. His furniture was antique Cherrywood. The leather sofa was beyond immaculate and neither D'Shawn nor Lee had a clue of whether they were permitted to sit, for the opulence left them indecisive and reluctant. Bobby sensed their perplexity and waved them the okay to sit down in the cocaine plush comfortable chairs in front of his desk.

"Okay Lee, you're probably wantin' to know what's on my mind and like always, business," Bobby explained with his hands clamped together.

On his fingers, he had some scintillating gold rings that, too, looked antique.

This Arab got more than I expected, D'Shawn thought, as well as Lee, who was judging from the same perspective.

"I see that you guys have moved on to big things in life. A man and his crew doesn't pull up to where he started in .745, and not be doing big things," said Bobby, simultaneously typing away on his computer. When he was done he turned the computer monitor around so that D'Shawn and Lee could see the screen.

"How would you like to do business in this area?" Bobby asked.

D'Shawn and Lee both stared at the semi-automatic assault rifles and both liked what they were seeing.

"AK47 made fully, all the way to tommy gun .45. You name it and the Arab got it," said Bobby advertising his artillery.

D'Shawn and Lee both knew that they would need no more ammunition than what they had stored at their trap house on 129th and Kentucky. *The dope game is for nobody to get too comfortable and think that they were not subject to a visit by the Jack boys,* D'Shawn thought.

The Stash is getting taller every day, and what money doesn't bring problems? Lee thought.

"How much you want for five AK's and a Mac-10 with an additional five Glock .21?" D'Shawn asked Bobby.

"I can tell you're related to Lee, so I'mma treat you like him... for you Jenkins boys, two hundred a piece and free access to my shooting range," said Bobby.

"Deal, we can't beat that... now we need some wheels for half price, Bobby," Lee said frankly.

"Deal buddy," Bobby said, grateful for the good business that Lee had always brought him.

The AK47s are comin' straight from Saudi Arabia custom made, fully automatic for all of the firearms. What's a team without a good connect?... Easy Prey, thought D'Shawn.

———

When Varshay made it to the parking lot, she was excited to be finally going home for the day. Her science class had her in extreme exhaustion and all she wanted to do was go home and get some rest. She could feel the comfort of her bed at every step she took in the ardent sun. As she got closer to her car, she saw the silhouette of a figure in the vicinity, but couldn't make out the person, 'cause of the beaming sun in her eyes. It wasn't until she was at the car next to hers that she saw the last person that she'd expected to see ever again.

"What the fuck you want, T-Mac?!" Varshay bitterly asked with extreme spitefulness in her tone.

This bitch out her mind, T-Mac wanted to say, but kept his cool.

"Damn Varshay, what's all this about?" T-Mac asked calmly and sadly.

"I don't have shit to say to you. Point blank," Varshay retorted sternly.

"So that's how we are?"

"Fuck you, T-Mac! I hate you and I don't want shit to do with yo' dog ass, nigga. Leave me alone, okay!" Varshay screamed out then stormed past T-Mac to get inside her car.

When she passed him, T-Mac grabbed ahold of her wrist vigorously and pulled her into his chest in an embrace. Not caring who was looking, T-Mac forced his lips to hers and his tongue in her mouth.

"Ummmmmm!" Varshay resisted his kiss by pulling away from him and spit saliva out her mouth onto the ground.

"Let me go, nigga!" Varshay screamed hysterically, trying to free herself from his embrace but it was a death grip.

"Get off her!" Yalunder screamed hitting T-Mac in the back of his head with her school books.

Yeah, hit his ass, girl, Varshay thought, seeing the look on T-Mac's face from the blow. She hit him twice with one of them get ya mind right science books. T-Mac let Varshay go and tried to backhand Yalunder. She immersed and T-Mac's hand was caught in the midst of his intentions. He was shocked and startled when he turned around to see Tony P holding his wrist in a death grip and a menacing look on his face.

"Nigga, I wish you would put your hands on mines," Tony P said between clenched teeth, then vigorously pushed T-Mac to the ground. When T-Mac hit the ground, Tony tried to follow up and pounce on T-Mac. But he was stopped short when Varshay and Yalunder jumped in his path to restrain him.

"No Tony P, he not worth it!!" screamed Varshay.

"Pussy nigga, you dead, homie... you dead!" T-Mac shouted out, after coming back to his feet.

"T-Mac, just go! Please! Go now!" Varshay turned around in rage.

"Baby no, no, no!" Yalunder cried out, hugging Tony P.

The commotion caused students who were down with the star quarterback to come at his aid. When T-Mac saw he support he made the wise decision of departing ways.

"I'mma see you, fuck boy!" said T-Mac.

"Yeah, just know Tony P ain't doing no runnin', B!"

"We'll see nigga," T-Mac said, then stormed off at the sight of security approaching. Everyone scattered like rats, and got in their cars to avoid security.

T-Mac's entire drive back to the hood he only had two niggas on his mind. And he would deal with them like any other nigga that stepped in his way.

"Varshay is my bitch!" T-Mac shouted out to no one but himself.

He wasn't about to let no nigga get away with takin' his bitch from him or putting their hands on him.

Tony P, you done cross that line homie! T-Mac thought as he accelerated to the hood.

CHAPTER 9

DESPITE HER DAY being a complete wreck from T-Mac's unexpected visit. She was now at peace and in the arms that were promising to always protect her. D'Shawn was upset when she'd told him the news and badly wanted to step to T-Mac personally just to set the record straight. D'Shawn was furious, but Varshay had talked him out of it, knowing that T-Mac wasn't worth the trouble. Her parents had no clue of D'Shawn's presence in their home, and had no right to just come into her room unexpected, either.

I can't wait until I'm eighteen years old so that I can move into my own shit, Varshay thought as D'Shawn held her from the back. Looking at the clock on her nightstand's illuminating red digital numbers, she saw that it was 4:02 AM, and D'Shawn was asleep.

Even in the bed, he doesn't make attempts to make a move against me. I want to feel him inside of me... damn! It's been a while, Varshay thought, sexually frustrated. D'Shawn's patience deep down turned her on. He was the first to ever treat her special and she would wait until he was ready. Slowly, she reversed herself and snuggled up against D'Shawn, awaking him. When she opened his eyes, she pecked him on his lips.

"What time is it?" D'Shawn asked embracing Varshay tightly.

"Almost time for me to get up. My mom would be in here soon to remind me," Varshay explained.

"Well I'm goin' to leave, but I'll be back at 6:00."

"Why?" Varshay asked confounded.

"I'm taking you to school and picking you up."

"Oh yeah?" Varshay said raising out of bed with D'Shawn.

"I have to pee... Be back," Varshay said hurriedly.

When she walked towards the bathroom sashaying in her mini t-shirt and black satin thongs. D'Shawn couldn't resist the erection as he watched her flawless yellow succulent ass cheeks jiggle with every step she took. *Damn that bitch really fuckin my head up.*

As much as D'Shawn wanted to fuck her, he still felt it would be perfect to wait it out for her birthday. She was his bitch and despite her telling him not to worry about it, he was still going to step down on T-Mac, whenever he saw him. There was a line of respect that had to be stipulated, because if a nigga didn't know, then no man could be upset. When Varshay came out of the bathroom D'Shawn had his clothes on and was ready to go. He walked up to Varshay and gave her a passionate, sloppy kiss, causing her to let out a moan.

"Ummm!"

"I'll be back at 6:00AM okay," D'Shawn whispered. The kiss had her moonstruck and speechless and her pussy extremely wet, as she rubbed her hands on his muscular chest, salaciously.

"You okay, baby?"

"Yes D'Shawn, I'm okay. I'll be ready, but we have to at least get some breakfast before school. I can stand a tardy, so don't worry," said Varshay, still rubbing D'Shawn's chest.

"Whatever you want to do baby..."

Fuck the shit out of you. Varshay badly wanted to say. "Okay," she retorted.

Varshay walked towards the window and raised it to let D'Shawn out into the morning atmosphere. He kissed her once more before he vanished into the darkness. She instantly heard her mom in the kitchen preparing to cook for her father, something that was routine.

One day I'll be able to cook for D'Shawn, Varshay thought as she pulled back down the window then strutted over, climbing back into bed. Trying to catch sleep was out of the question. All she could think about was D'Shawn making love to her. Unable to resist the sensation forming between her legs, she took her moist thong off and rubbed her throbbing clitoris with her eyes closed. She envisioned D'Shawn stroking her from behind, thrusting deep inside her love box.

"D'Shawn baby!" She moaned out in a whisper, rubbing her clitoris rapidly. When she came, she came with a convulsive electrifying orgasm that put her straight to sleep.

———

When D'Shawn pulled up to his family rowhouse, he saw that his mom had company, someone that D'Shawn deeply hated and couldn't see why his mom even dealt with this nigga. Since his dad caught life in prison, his mom had fallen in love with a straight busta, named Alex. Alex weighed at the least 350lbs and dressed like an oily ass junkie. D'Shawn knew his mom was only interested in Alex's money he made as a truck driver. One day he and Alex had gotten into a quarrel about the food supply in the house. When she saw that Alex had an indifference liking against him, D'Shawn warned Alex to stay out his way. Alex, being a prudent man, and knowing his stepson's reputation stayed in his place and wisely out of D'Shawn's way.

When D'Shawn stepped foot in the house, he found his mom sitting in the living room on the worn-down leather sofa alone, watching TV, and Alex snoring loudly from the back room they shared.

"Hey mama, you up early."

"Yeah, can't sleep with that whale in the backroom," Connie said while smoking on a Newport 100 cigarette.

"Yeah I feel ya, is everything okay?" D'Shawn asked sensing his mom's mental disturbance.

"Can I have a word with you, son?" Connie asked, exhaling smoke from her mouth and nostrils.

"Yeah Ma, I'm all ears," D'Shawn retorted taking the seat next to his mom.

"Son, I see you, Lee, and Leon wearing fly gear, and we know how y'all out there stealing cars. Now you pullin' up in a .745 BMW. Boy, I ain't no fool. Your daddy was the same way. Do you know where he went wrong?" Connie asked, pulling on the cigarette, and exhaling simultaneously. D'Shawn sat quietly, and waited until she was ready to speak again.

She was hitting on something that he'd been dying to know. *Where did his dad go wrong when the system took him away when I was only four years old?* D'Shawn wanted to know, and Connie told him, heartbroken.

"He was getting plenty money, and mama was the last person on his mind, D'Shawn... he left mama for dead," Connie said as the tears cascaded from her eyes.

It was painful to see his mom cry. She was a strong woman, five-feet-five-inches, caramel, 125lbs with a heart like a giant. Despite having trust issues with her when it came to financial dealings, he had no right to leave her out. He'd been so caught up in trying to satisfy himself that he was neglecting the woman who'd brought him into this world. *Damn how fucked up money could make you look,* D'Shawn thought. He was wordless, and deeply in pain.

"D'Shawn, I'm not telling you what to do with your money. But, always remember that when everyone else leaves at the sound of the storm... mama goin' to still be there," Connie said, getting up from the worn-down sofa and walking back to her room, leaving D'Shawn alone in his shamefulness. When he heard the door close, he held his head down in disappointment.

I may have trust issues with her when it comes to money, but I couldn't leave my mom in the storm, D'Shawn thought, unaware that a storm had already broken his mom. Mother's Day was next month and he would make sure that he took care of mom. D'Shawn went to his room and counted out $20,000 from his stash spot. He put the $20,000 in a big envelope addressed to his mom. It was 5:45 AM when he hopped out the shower and quickly dressed in an all-black True religion outfit, and some black and grey Jordan's No.23. Before he left the house, he slid the envelope under his mom's door.

"Mama!" He called out.

"Yeah?"

"Look in that envelope... It's fo' you" D'Shawn said then left feeling better about himself that he'd taken care of Mama. He couldn't wait for Mother's Day to come so he could show his deep appreciation for the woman that brought him into this world.

Varshay loved the BMW and its luxurious material. Trey Songz emanated from the car system at a low volume, and put her in a more splendid mood. Looking at D'Shawn maneuver through traffic calm and collect turned her on.

In his ashtray, he had a phat purple haze blunt and she assumed that he was waiting until she got out his sight to burn it. Varshay only tried smoking marijuana twice, both times with T-Mac, and she enjoyed the relaxed feelin' it gave her. *He could at least fog the car and let me catch second hand contact,* Varshay thought.

When they pulled up to the IHOP restaurant, she was anticipating getting her grub on. Together, they walked in like a couple, and sat themselves at a back, corner booth, alone by themselves in the vicinity.

"What would you two be ordering today? It's a special on pancakes and sausages if you buy more than five each," the heavy-set, black middle-aged waitress said, who was extremely dark skinned. D'Shawn looked at Varshay, who looked as if she was lost at what to get herself.

"Baby, if you want to eat the entire IHOP we could afford it, so get what you want. What you get it'll settle for me as well, baby," said D'Shawn, sensing her inquiry of limitations.

"Okayyy!" Varshay said with a blushful sigh.

D'Shawn smiled as Varshay ordered a lengthy breakfast for them. Together, they stuffed their faces in silence, unabashed of eating piggishly in front of each other. When they were done, they both left, gratified of the delicious breakfast. Inside, Varshay wasted no time grabbing the blunt from the ashtray.

"Lighter please," said Varshay holding her hand out with the blunt in her mouth, D'Shawn smiled at Varshay's bad girl attitude and reached in his pocket to retrieve his unique pistol designed lighter. With one pull on the trigga, the flame shot out, lighting the blunt. Varshay pulled deeply on the blunt, exhaling all the smoke, only inhaling a little and coughing. She passed the blunt to D'Shawn, trying to bridle her cough, and became instantly high.

"That's it... one hit?" D'Shawn asked with a smirk.

"That's all I need, something I've been tryin' to tell you since last night!" Varshay said, throwing a curveball at D'Shawn, who caught it with a smile on his face.

"Trust me... you'll have your shot... trust me boo," said D'Shawn sincerely.

━━

T-Mac, Bean, and Chase all sat in their stash house counting money and coming to conclusions of setting more runners in some of their traps. Every six months, T-Mac had a routine rotating of men in his traps. The heroin game was too sweet for him, and he was ready to put his foot down in other sections of Newark, something that the small-time hustlers weren't doing. Which made it no competition. But now he had a small crew that was putting up comparable numbers.

"I say we lay all that shit down, T-Mac," said Chase.

"Yeah, nip that shit in the bud before it become too outrageous."

"B, that nigga ain't no threat to Bean, damn!" Bean said, ready to get on some war shit.

"Listen, we ain't even goin' to sweat them niggas. Real niggas will sell a nigga what he askin' fo'. If they sellin' crack, we go buy it by the kilo and shut what they got down."

"And what if they ain't sellin' us no kilo, B?" Asked Bean, cutting T-Mac off.

"Then we war with them pussy ass niggas," said T-Mac, taking a swig from his fifth of Hennessy bottle.

"So, what you got on yo mind 'bout that nigga Tony P?" Asked Bean.

"Let me handle Tony P," T-Mac retorted.

D'Shawn, Lee and Leon were in their trap houses on 129th and Kentucky, all of them focused on their job. D'Shawn was in the kitchen breaking down a kilo of cocaine, rocked up after being cooked just last night. There was a million pieces of dime-sized crack scattered on the glass table. He'd went through with multiple razor blades, cutting the crack to perfection. D'Shawn and his cousins' spread was now all the way down to 159th and Boston, with trap houses on each street, if not runners in the dope holes. They had a team of go-getters moving packs of crack faster than the runners had time to count his quantity of capsules in his Ziploc bag. Leon was busy counting up all the cash in the living room, while Lee placed the crack in capsules to have them ready to go.

After what D'Shawn had done for his mother, he had encouraged Lee and Leon to do the same thing. They both gave their mom $15,000 a piece, then gave Grandma Patty Queen $15,000, along with D'Shawn. As D'Shawn cut the crack to dimes, he had a vision of being the man himself. He wanted to one day be in Skip's spot, to be able to hand over a kilo of cocaine like nothing. *As long as we stack this money, we will be able to be more than Skip, D'Shawn thought* unaware of his addiction not being distinctive from a fiend's. And unaware that he still had a lot to learn, before he could reach Skip's status.

Soon, we'll have to go looking for us a lowkey spot before we get too hot! Thought D'Shawn, ready to buy his own spot to lay his head and to call his own. The new ambition that was coming upon D'Shawn would sure enough capsize Skip's intentions for the ingenious trio. Borrowed time was of the essence, little did Skip know.

CHAPTER 10

SKIP WAS NOW GIVING the trio the heroin game cut and dry, straight up, as well as introducing them to the molly investment. He wanted these niggas to bring him 15% off of the molly distribution and 25% from the heroin.

"My nigga, we a team now and ain't no nigga in Jersey can pull out what we pullin' out. It ain't about sellin' for no nigga B, it's about standin' up wit' a nigga. I could've gave a lot of niggas the chance of an opportunity that I'm giving y'all. A nigga ain't powerin' up unless we allow them. These niggas gonna hustle, all y'all got to do it put it in their hands and make sure they come to y'all with the back end. Put the product out there and scrape off 25%. If a nigga not feelin' the stipulations... wash 'em B, and set an example," Skip advised his crew in the living room of his luxurious palace.

He loved how the trio listened attentively, because it meant the he had them right where he wanted them, focused. In all actuality, they were the only ones that had to pay a percentage off of what he put in their hands. He did it so connivingly bold the he made the prospect seem real to the ingenious crew. He had a strong connect, and some killers down with him, but he'd never come close to extorting any of his clientele. He made it seem as if every hustler in

Jersey had to pay him a percentage just to hustle. And the trio believed him thoroughly.

These niggas ducks, and would bring me every nigga in the streets' percentage, thought Skip. To them, he was only expecting 15% and 25% between the molly and heroin. Other niggas were breaking him off 50%. As shocking as it was them, he was still able to deceive the trio.

"D'Shawn, I'mma make you my right-hand man, Vice General and you two," Skip said, pointing at Lee and Leon. "Y'all are my two wardens of the streets. In no time, these niggas will get with the program and see that it's a new Newark movement," said Skip.

Something don't smell right 'bout none of it, but I can't explain why I feel like I do! D'Shawn thought. When he looked at Lee and Leon, he saw the rapacious ambition on their faces. *We 'bout to take this shit to another level, we definitely need a lowkey spot,* thought D'Shawn.

"You okay, D'Shawn?" Skip asked, breaking D'Shawn's train of thought. D'Shawn looked up and downed the last of his glass of Hennessy, then said sincerely.

"I'm ready to regulate, and I mean every day, B."

⸺

"Oh my gosh baby!" Yalunder purred out as Tony P penetrated her excessive wet pussy. He had her legs on his right shoulder as he pounded his large dick into her on his king-sized bed.

"Beat this pussy... uhhh shit I love this dick!" She shouted out in ecstasy.

Tony P had no football practice today and had been ready to fuck his main bitch for two weeks now. He still hadn't told her the good news, that he'd received last week, nor anyone else. Receiving a full scholarship for the University of Miami was what he'd been praying for all year. He just didn't know how he was going to tell Yalunder that he was going away. He loved Yalunder and had been her boyfriend since 9th grade. But he knew what temptation he had waiting on him in Miami, and he didn't want to deal with the headache of a long distance relationship. He would have to let Yalunder go. A thought that was far from contemplation.

"Baby, em cumming!" Yalunder purred loudly in ecstasy as she orgasmed for the third time.

"Arghhh!" Tony P grunted, pulling his dick out and shooting his warm load on Yalunder's stomach.

Why did he pull out? Yalunder thought.

She hated when Tony P pulled out instead of sending his load through her tunnel. She had no clue, nor asked Tony P for an explanation. All she knew was that she loved him to death and one day would bear his children. She felt that entrapping him with a kid would forever have him in her life; either in her bed, or deep in his pockets.

When D'Shawn had talked to the real estate agent an hour ago to look at a five-bedroom home in West Orange, New Jersey, he didn't think that she was actually a black woman, and furthermore, a gorgeous black woman at that. Her name was Brittany James, and she resembled Kelly Rowland in the face, and Beyoncé in the body. The suit that she wore accentuated her curvaceous Coke bottle frame.

"Hello, Mr. Jenkins, I'm glad that you could make it," Brittany exclaimed as she offered her hand. D'Shawn pumped her hand gently.

"I'm glad you've made it too, Ms. James."

They were standing out front the home, both admiring each other's conspicuous vehicles. Brittany had a 5-class pearl white Benz and D'Shawn couldn't help but acknowledge this boss bitch.

"Good, well let me show you the inside," Brittany said then sashayed towards the front door of the beautiful home. The clanking of her heels resounded as she walked inside the empty, immaculate, spacious home.

"This is the living room that's adjunct to the den, Mr. Jenkins."

"Call me D'Shawn," D'Shawn said, preferring for her to call him by his first name.

"And just call me Brittany," she retorted.

"Deal," D'Shawn said, looking at Brittany with burning lust in his eyes that was evident to her. She was used to it, and continued her tour. She gave D'Shawn a tour of the entire house on the inside, then took him to the spacious back yard, that had a 15ft pool. He already had it in his mind that he was going to purchase the home the moment he saw it. He surveyed the neighbors and saw that they were all the same...white.

"So what do you think, D'Shawn?" Brittany asked seductively.

"I think that you too beautiful for me to say no," D'Shawn retorted, causing Brittany to blush with a big smile. D'Shawn was perplexed. Was it his comment on her scintillating beauty, or because she'd sold her house to him.

"Thank you for coming, just call me when you are ready," Brittany said.

"I'll be ready tonight," D'Shawn said as they walked back through the empty house, locking the house back up, then walking out to their cars as Brittany explained the protocol. The ass she had wasn't bigger than Varshay's, but that didn't stop him from lusting.

▭

Skip had been waiting on his connect to call him back with the location of the drop site. In the meantime, he was wrapping half kilo of heroin in plastic and duct tape. One of his runners had got picked up by the Jakes and was now back on the streets three days later.

"A nigga don't get knocked with a half of that boy then let loose three days later. I want him gone before sunrise," Skip ordered the young nigga E-Money, who'd been putting in work for Skip for a while now. If Skip wanted a nigga slumped, then he had his goons like E-Money who had an innumerable count of bodies.

"You'll get the other half when it's done," said Skip, handing E-Money the half kilo of heroin.

"Say no mo, that nigga will be gone before midnight," E-Money exclaimed.

"Great, because that's what I need B, can't trust that nigga," said Skip.

When E-Money was gone, Skip walked to his room and got back into bed with Tracy, who had been waiting for him to return, so that she could give him some more mind-blowing head. She looked every bit of Roxy Reynolds the exotic model/dancer. Skip came out his black wife beater and gym shorts, then climbed in bed with Tracy.

"Daddy's back, huh?" Tracy exclaimed as she grabbed a hold of Skip's throbbing dick, then immersed beneath the covers, taking him in her mouth. Skip's toes instantly curled into a fetal position.

"Damn baby, that shit feels good," Skip purred. Tracy sped her pace simultaneously, skillfully stroking him as she sucked his dick. T-Mac had been blowing her phone up, but she'd been too busy with Skip to answer. And to Tracy, good dick and money always came before a nigga in her world. *Especially one who was stuck on a bad breakup with a young girl who was so over him,* thought Tracy as she deep throated Skip.

━━━

E-Money had watched Joel come back in forth to the corner store at least five times in one hour. The Arab corner store in East Orange on 27th and Bowling stayed accessible until 2:00AM. It was only 11:00PM, and Joel was in the store purchasing another swiss cigar and cheap ass Budweiser. Only a few niggas were hanging outside, and had seen E-Money's face, but he wasn't worried, because East Orange lived on a strong street code. There were no snitches, and everyone was skeptical of Joel.

As he saw Joel at the register paying for his items, E-Money walked to the side of the store, which was an alley, and pretended to be pissing. With a black hoodie sweater over his head like he was in as much disguise as he could be. When E-Money heard the bells ringing on the door, indicating someone exiting or entering, he knew it was Joel. E-Money pulled out his Glock .40, racked it, then waited until he saw Joel come towards his direction. When Joel strutted past him, E-Money aimed at the back of Joel's head and pulled the trigger.

Boom! Boom! Boom! The shots made everyone scatter frantically like roaches. When E-Money saw that it was clear, he emerged from the dead-end alley and counted Joel's death as fifty on his body count. E-Money was a skinny six-foot-one, peanut butter assassin from Camden, New Jersey. The perpetual murder capital in Jersey. Murder for hire was all he did and would get flipped triple the going price in East Orange, and Newark. Due to the drought in Camden, E-Money was 'bout to make a tremendous profit.

"Say them boyz on da block sell anything fo' profit. Five in the morning on the corner clockin'!" E-Money serenaded to the lyrics of rapper Jody Breeze from the *Boyz in the Hood* hit, as he accelerated his conspicuous Cherry Red Dodge Charger gingerly back to Camden to lay low and shut it down in its vulnerable stage.

━━━

Leon had just left Nicole's house in Camden, NJ. He'd won the two hundred dollars against D'Shawn when he came back with the number of the bad bitch in the pink Range Rover at "Bobby's Rims". And now, he was the happiest man in Newark after just fucking her to complete exhaustion. He was on molly and could fuck a line long of hoes right about now. He soon found out that Nicole was in the dope game, as well as holding her boyfriend/clientele down until he finished serving time in the Trenton State Penitentiary. He had five years until he would even be considered for parole options. In the meantime, Leon planned to fuck Nicole on every corner he had an opportunity to. The bitch had some good pussy, and he couldn't wait to tell Lee and D'Shawn. What Leon didn't know was that he was fucking with a boss bitch. *That bitch looks every bit of Tyga's baby mom Blac Chyna and can suck a mean dick,* Leon thought as he pulled up to the Arab store on 129th and Kentucky.

Before he went to the trap house, he needed to grab a box of Swisher Sweet cigars. It was a couple niggas just out hanging around trying to make a dollar. They were all Leon's workers who he'd brought from nothing to something.

"What's good, Leon?" one of his workers named Smokey asked as Leon walked towards the front door.

"What's up B, just cooling it," Leon retorted as he pumped Smokey's hand. Smoke was a twenty-one-year-old go-getta who made sure that the money from the junkies was always straight, no penny or dollar less, because all money wasn't money in Smokey's eyes.

When Leon walked into the Arab store he saw his homie T Gutta who'd just hopped out the pen and was already getting in where he fitted in on 129th and Kentucky. Leon just hoped the nigga stayed free and didn't let the jakes catch him with anymore drugs. T Gutta was happy to see Leon walk into the store.

"What's up, nigga!?"

"You tell me B, you home and pockets already lumped up," Leon retorted, pumping T Gutta's hand and embracing him in a welcome home hug.

"Yeah man, I'mma stay out h—"

Boc! Boc! Boc!

"Ohh shit B!" Leon screamed as he ran down an aisle to cover from any stray bullets. T Gutta ran out the store to join the niggas doing the drive-by, by squeezing off two Glock .40's at the fleeing SUV.

Boom! Boom! Boc! Boc! Boom! Boom! Boom!

Leon wasn't about to let only his workers hold down 129th and Kentucky. He ran out the store and round off at the fleeing SUV also with his Glock .21

Boom! Boom! Boom! Leon made a dash, simultaneously squeezing rapidly at the bold SUV tail lights. The SUV turned on 136th and Texas and was gone.

"Fuck!" Leon shouted frustratingly, holding his smoking Glock .21.

When he came back towards the store to investigate the scenery, he found two of his niggas dead. One of them was Smokey, who was taken first. He was slouched down on the wall bullet riddled. Next to him, a couple feet away, laid young T Ray slain at seventeen years old.

"Fuck!!"

Leon became furious as he looked at his homies slumped in front of the Arab store, and received a revelation at the same time. He had enough money to supply all his runners with pistols and put a watchman on each block. He didn't know what triggered someone to come gun down his workers, but in his gut, he thought he knew what the provocation was. And if his conclusion was accurate, then he had more to worry about. D'Shawn and Lee were hitting his phone at the same time. He knew that they were calling to check up on him.

"Yo, T Gutta get from up here, Jakes comin!" Leon ordered, T Gutta as they both heard distant sirens intensifying.

"Okay B," T Gutta said then hopped in an all-black Charger, leaving the scene. Leon did the same thing by hopping in his BMW saying fuck the cigars. Once inside and behind the wheel, he answered the phone and spoke to D'Shawn.

"What's good nigga, you in the area?"

"I'm on my way B, somebody just got Smokey and T Ray!!" Leon said, cutting D'Shawn off.

"Dammit!" D'Shawn exclaimed, "D.O.S.?" D'Shawn asked.

"Yeah, both of them," Leon said, disconnecting the call as he pulled up to the trap.

Bean and Chase had quickly gotten rid of the stolen bullet riddled Dodge Durango on 26th street in the meat house parking lot inconspicuously. On foot, they both walked back to 33rd using every alley and pathway furtively.

"I think that was Smokey, B," Chase said.

"Well, too bad bra was out there. I don't know of any slug that has names on them in drive-by's, Blood," Bean retorted.

"True," Chase agreed.

Him and Bean had just done a drive-by on 129th and Kentucky, just for the fun of it. And since there was unspoken animosity amongst them and 129th and Kentucky, Bean decided to seize the opportunity to kick off war first. But T-Mac wouldn't know anything of it, he'll be in perplexity just like everyone else was. *They have no clue who did the fatal shooting, Blatt!* Bean thought, as he sauntered through the darkness, with an addition to his body count.

CHAPTER 11

THE PROM OCCURRING on her birthday was the best gift she'd received thus far. Standing in her dresser top mirror embellishing herself, Varshay was nervous and anxious to see her father's reaction to D'Shawn. Him being an ol'school austere man, you didn't know what to expect out of him. Varshay observed how beautiful she looked in her Vera Wang dress that her father had purchased her custom made at a costly figure. Her pearls accentuated a queenly woman and they too were costly.

"You look beautiful, baby girl," her father said, startling her as he stood in the doorway, with a cup of Hennessy in his hands.

She had no clue that her father deep down was experiencing an unwanted revelation of losing his daughter to a street nigga. His expectations for her were higher than she'd ever know. But far from seeing her in love with a fuckin' street thug. Her father looked like the twin brother to Colin Powell, and he moved in aspiration just like the Secretary of State, four-star, retired general.

"How long have you been standin' there, daddy?" Varshay asked while touching up on her makeup.

"Just a minute... like I came to request a minute of your time!" her father said as he walked into her room and took a seat on her plush bed.

"Well, I have more than a minute for my father," said Varshay putting a smile on her father's face. A smile that was more feigned than the tooth fairy, and one Varshay noticed instantly.

He's stressin', I can see it all in his wrinkled forehead! Varshay thought, while watching him through the reflection in the mirror.

"What's wrong daddy?" Varshay turned around asking her father. When she saw the tears in the wells of his eyes and his bottom lip trembling, it pained her. *I ain't never seen my daddy cry...damn!* Varshay thought.

"Father...what's wrong?" Varshay asked her father, already knowing the answer, then sat next to her father on the bed.

"Baby I want you to always know that daddy going to always be here for you," he paused to wipe the tears that had finally fallen from the wells of his eyes, then grabbed Varshay's hand gently.

"Baby girl... I can't tell you how to live your life but just be careful out there. It's plenty more to learn beyond being eighteen, baby. Don't fall in them streets, Varshay," he said taking a sip from his cup of Hennessy. "Remember that no man loves you more than daddy, Varshay!!"

"I will always remember daddy."

"Varshay, your date is here!!" Varshay's mother Melina shouted from the living room.

Varshay looked in her father's eyes and saw the negative energy forming within him. But he was no one to judge any man that his daughter loved. *She grown now,* he thought.

"Well let's let 2Pac take my baby to a prom, not to a shootout."

"Daddy. Stop with the insults, please!" Varshay said sternly and fed up with her father's critics on her choice of men. *For God's sake, I'm fucking eighteen now!* She thought. Before her dad could explode tempestuously, he bridled himself and walked out the room to go meet his daughter's date. When he saw D'Shawn standing at the front door in an all-white immaculate Versace suit, with a dozen of red roses in his hands, all thoughts of a thug vanished.

This man looks like a business man, or at least he's covered himself up as one, thought Marvin.

"How are you this evening, Mr. Lewis?" D'Shawn spoke.

He has no golds in his mouth, maybe he a damn geek thug, Marvin thought wanting to chuckle at his thoughts of D'Shawn.

"Pleasure to meet you D'Shawn," Marvin said spurious.

"Don't expect that formality speech from me son, just enjoy yourself tonight and make it an indelibly night, son," Marvin spoke.

"I will sir, and it's a dyin' pleasure to meet you and Mrs. Lewis as well. I assure you that we will have fun, Mr. Lewis."

I bet you will, geek thug, Mr. Marvin Lewis thought and badly wanted to say. *But then he might get mad and pull a gun out to gun me down,* Marvin considered.

On the other hand, Mrs. Lewis was fond of D'Shawn's benignity and saw him as a nice young man. It was evident to D'Shawn where Varshay got her beauty from. Her and her mom had some striking resemblance. *Mom dukes a straight "Dime Piece Diva,"* D'Shawn thought when he first saw her. When D'Shawn saw Varshay come into the living room, he noticed just how radiant and mettlesome she was. He was astounded at her scintillating beauty. The sky-blue Vera Wang dress with the sexy ass slit in the front accentuated all of her delicate curves. Varshay, smiling bright, walked right into D'Shawn's arms.

"These are for you, happy birthday baby," he said as he kissed Varshay gently on her cheeks, then hand, before handing her the roses.

Mrs. Lewis wasted no time flashing a rapid session of pictures with her Kodak camera. She had a mother's joy all over her face wiping tears away. While Mr. Lewis stood with his hands in his pockets putting on a feigned smile, for the sake of Varshay.

"Thank you so much, D'Shawn... I'm sure you've met my

parents, acourse you have. But I still want to introduce you to them myself. This is my mom Melina Lewis and my dad Mr. Marvin Lewis," Varshay spoke nervously and dying to fluctuate atmospheres. One absent of her parents. She was swarming with butterflies.

"Okay you two, stand over by that wall so I can get a picture before you two leave," Mrs. Lewis said as she guided the duo to the ornate wall. Together they took a couple pictures, as Varshay clung to D'Shawn's arm. He just knew that he was about to step in West Orange High with the most toothsome, gorgeous, breathtaking woman in the building.

"Well I don't want to keep y'all waiting. Let me put these roses in some water for you, baby. They'll be in your room when you come back," Mrs. Lewis said grabbing the roses from Varshay.

"Thanks mom, and goodnight to the both of y'all. I love you," Varshay exclaimed, simultaneously hugging her parents and giving them a goodnight kiss.

"Be safe you two," Mr. Lewis said, as he opened the door for the twosome.

"We will," the twosome said in unison.

When Varshay proceeded out the front door she was slammed awestruck as she stared at the all-white conspicuous Hummer limousine.

"Oh my gosh D'Shawn!!" Varshay exclaimed in deep astonishment, covering her mouth with her hands. *I give him high ratings on this one. At least he's not taking my baby to prom in some loud ghetto ass tricked out SUV or car,* Mr. Lewis thought, who as well was awestruck.

"What did you think that we were going to half step on my baby birthday, and prom night?" D'Shawn spoke while he offered his arm so that Varshay could intertwine and be walked to the limp queenly. When the duo made it to the back door of the limo, the black muscular chauffeur opened the door, and Varshay immediately saw Tony P and Yalunder waiting on her too, with a candle lit chocolate cake in the palms of their hands.

"Happy Birthday, Varshay!!" her friends screamed in unison.

"Oh my gosh, how many mo' surprises, D'Shawn?!" Varshay shouted ecstatically.

"Every moment of tonight will be 'bout you baby, so get prepared fo' the ride. We goin' beyond exhaustion baby," D'Shawn exclaimed, throwing a curve ball at Varshay who caught it with a smile.

"Oh really, beyond exhaustion huh!?" Varshay said seductively.

"Girl, get yo' ass in so we could go and blow out these candles 'cause they makin' me hot!" Yalunder exclaimed.

"Please do, 'cause I'm tired of hearing her mouth and she ain't even drunk yet." Tony P said causing everyone to erupt in laughter, including Yalunder.

"Whateverr... you a clown!" Yalunder spat.

D'Shawn and Varshay stepped into the Hummer H2 and melted in each other's arms instantly, enjoying the opulence of the limo. She blew all eighteen candles out and cut everyone a large slice of cake. D'Shawn pressed a button on the roof and allowed the sun roof to slide back, revealing a beautiful sky illuminated with a full moon, and precious stars. He then pressed another button and from the deck of the limo ascended a round table with a champagne flute shelf attached to the side of the table. Everyone beside D'Shawn seemed amazed at the uniqueness of the limo. D'Shawn pull out four champagne flutes and a bottle of Perignon that he pulled from under the seat. The champagne was chilled, and relaxing for the foursome.

Bitches might pull up in limousines, but not no stretch Hummer limos. I don't think that T-Mac would've made an appearance like this. D'Shawn is a different breed from the ordinary street nigga. This nigga is an extraordinary street nigga who knows how to treat a woman. Tonight, he had no excuses because. By all means, I will take that dick tonight.

"What's on your mind?" D'Shawn asked Varshay interrupting, her thoughts, knowing when she was engrossed in dep thought. Instead of an answer, Varshay leaned into D'Shawn and kissed him passionately.

"I know that's right girl!" Yalunder exclaimed as Tony P held her in a warming embrace, watching Varshay kiss the man of her happiness.

"I was just thinking handsome... no excuses tonight, right?" Varshay asked D'Shawn, feeling the moisture to her sultry mound between her legs intensify, soaking her satin thongs.

"Acourse, there are no excuses... and no mercy," D'Shawn retorted, sincerely.

She sat on the bathroom floor stuck in her own world. Her man was out of town like usual and she was praying for no surprise visits to ruin her time alone. Every light in the house was out, and the illuminated light in the bathroom come from a cheap dollar store candle. The smell of urine reeked badly, and hit her nose every time she inhaled her breath. She closed her eyes and was hit with another wave of overwhelmed depression. Her life was a complete wreck, and she only had one person to blame. And that was herself, sad to say, because she should've never been careless. She'd cried until she fell asleep, but the pain refused to subside and was always there when she awoke.

How could I be so dumb and not protect myself? She thought as the tears cascaded down her face.

She only knew of one way to subside the pain momentarily despite it being the main reason she was now HIV positive. She pulled out the capsule that contained the gram of heroin and placed it on a silver tablespoon over the burning candle. When she saw the heroin form into a liquid, she transferred it into another dirty syringe. She shook the needle in her right hand, simultaneously opening and closing her left hand, looking desperately for a vein. She was filled with euphoria when she found the usual vein. Clumsily, she injected the heroin into her veins and let the heroin take all of her sadden pain away.

"Awww!!" she exhaled in ecstasy, pushing the needle to its capacity. She laid back against the dirty ring tub, drifting off to another world. A world where pain didn't exist.

━━

"So, when you gonna tell her 'bout your scholarship, B?" D'Shawn asked Tony P while they had the limited alone time amongst themselves until Varshay and Yalunder returned from the ladies' restroom. The prom was crowded with many couples dressed to their best expensive attire. A lot of envious females were upset when Varshay was crowned as their prom queen. But couldn't do shit about another woman's genuine beauty.

"I don't know B, but tellin' her would be hard," said Tony P. "But I show don't plan on tellin' her tonight." Tony P retorted.

"Hell nawl... Fuck no B, is you crazy?!" D'Shawn exclaimed.

"My nigga, check it, I've known you my whole life, and I know where you are predestined to be. University of Miami, full scholarship, first round pick to the Dolphins because, B... Them niggas straight sorry. Just come back home and regulate that Jets uniform first chance you get nigga, fo' real," D'Shawn exclaimed.

"You already know I'mma come back home B, can't forget the home team, B," Tony P retorted, elated from the anxious feeling of playing ball at the University of Miami.

"Subject dropped, there they go," D'Shawn said, walking off to grab Varshay as she sashayed across the French tiled floor under the Italian chandeliers. *Damn she's beautiful,* thought D'Shawn, *and you're lucky to have her,* his conscience reminded him.

Every step she took with Yalunder by her side, heads from both sexualities stared her down in awe. It was hard not become moonstruck when looking at the most toothsome prom queen in the enormous auditorium adjunct to the school.

"Sorry we took so long but that restroom is—"

"It's okay baby," D'Shawn said, cutting Varshay off and

embracing her in his arms on cue with a Marvin Gay song emanating through the massive subwoofers.

"Can I have this dance, beautiful?" D'Shawn asked Varshay.

"Yes, you can handsome" she permitted.

Together the foursome took the floor and slow danced artistically. Varshay was amazed how well D'Shawn was equipped to slow dancing, along with Tony P.

"Baby, where did you learn to dance?" Varshay asked, D'Shawn. He looked at her in her eyes then looked over her shoulders, where he locked eyes with Yalunder, who was slow dancing with Tony P. Attentively, he stared into Yalunder's eyes who seemed to be communicating with him concisely. It was the look of lust and was confirmed when Yalunder mouthed off to him for only him to read her lips. *I want you...soon.*

"D'Shawn, damn you not—"

"Oh, damn baby...uhhh, I learned it from watching my grandfather, and the same place you learned it from," D'Shawn said to Varshay who'd snapped him out of his trance with her friend.

"And where did I learn it from?" Varshay asked.

"From your heart, follow your steps matching my beats and you figured it out, simple," D'Shawn said, taking Varshay for a perfectible spin.

"D'Shawn!" Varshay screamed as she fell back into his arms, afraid that the spin wouldn't succeed.

"I'm here baby, like I said, follow your heart," said D'Shawn, then kissed Varshay on her lips. They were in their own world.

"I am baby... I'm following my heart," Varshay retorted.

"Me too, and it has yet failed me beautiful," D'Shawn said, concisely.

When he looked over her shoulders once again he stared into the eyes of Yalunder. She blew him a kiss and absentmindedly, he blew her one back.

Damn that bitch got me breaking all the rules to the game,

D'Shawn thought, consequently, realizing that he'd just opened a door that neither of them should be walking through. It just wasn't right, and neither of them wanted to admit it.

CHAPTER 12

CLUB MAXELL in downtown West Orange, NJ was a variety mixture of Pop and R&B club. The after party of the prom had crammed the club with the birth of a wild night yet to come. Limousines pulled up and walked their dates in the enormous two floor club on the red carpet. Club Maxell was famous for its attendance of celebrities such as NFL, NBA players and Pop and R&B artists. You were bound to meet at least one celebrity every week doing it big in VIP.

Tonight, Pop singer Nick Jonas, one of the Jonas brothers was Maxell's special guest and was live on stage performing his new hit single "Jealous."

When the conspicuous Hummer HZ pulled in front of club Maxwell, cameras began flashing rapidly from every angle. It was thus far the best limelight capturing, captivating a lot of couples who were wishing to be inside.

"Oh my gosh, girl! Camera's, lights, action! Yalunder shouted as she stepped out of the limousine intertwined on Tony P's arm, looking like a gorgeous high yellow skin toned model, sashaying in her sparkling baby blue Tom Ford gown.

"Yeah girl, this bitch super swole!" Varshay said highly excited and ready to get her drink and party on.

D'Shawn walked his prom queen in the club as Nick Jonas was performing on stage, and walked straight to VIP. Tony P knew the settings of tonight, so there were no surprises in it for him, unlike Yalunder and Varshay. *This nigga is goin' straight to VIP*, Varshay thought as they entered the bottom floor VIP section with no problems.

The French antique furniture was adorable, suitable, and comfortable. Moments after the foursome took their seats on the rich leather red button seats, bartenders came in, two pairs of gorgeous blondes wearing extremely come fuck me booty shorts and stilettos strapped up to their mid-calves. The tops they had on did nothing to help their large tits from spilling out. *Damn, these bitches bad as hell!* D'Shawn thought.

"And what will you fellas be drinking on tonight!" one of the pretty blondes asked. She looked like a Hilary Duff and D'Shawn couldn't keep his eyes off her phat pussy bulging through her cherry red boy shorts. Good thing Varshay and Yalunder were engrossed in each other's verbosity, being loquacious. Or else he would have been busted for gawking at the gorgeous bartender named, Kimberly, who'd made a mental note to try her darn best of obtaining D'Shawn's number before he left the club. Kimberly was definitely eye fucking D'Shawn and Tony P agreed as well.

"Yeah, ummm... bring us two bottles of coconut Cîroc and a gallon of straight vodka and orange juice, and I mean pure $100 orange juice," D'Shawn said emphasizing. "None of that artificial shit," he retorted.

"Trust me, it's all real!" Kimberly said seductively, flexing her bulging pussy lips so that D'Shawn saw.

When he looked over at Tony P, Tony P winked his right eye, capturing everything D'Shawn had witnessed to his own disbelief. To rub the guilty conscience from his mind, D'Shawn reached out and pulled Varshay away from chatty Yalunder and sat her on his lap.

"Oh shit Tony P, maybe we need to turn our heads!" Yalunder shouted over the Flo-Rida song "This Is My House" serenading the club. She watched the two love birds as she snuggled up against Tony P.

"Nawl you good, Yalunder I just need a moment of her time," D'Shawn said while rubbing Varshay's ass.

"So, are you enjoying this beautiful night?" Asked D'Shawn staring Varshay in her adorable, content eyes.

"D'Shawn, I am havin' a splendid time, baby. I'm ready to get to—"

Before she could finish, D'Shawn closed his lips on hers and kissed her passionately, and deeply. Varshay wrapped her arms around his neck and intensified the kiss. Feeling the moisture between her legs made her want to give D'Shawn the pussy at that moment. D'Shawn must've sensed her tempted thought, because he eased up, to calm her fiery down.

"We have a long night baby, and I mean a long night!" D'Shawn shouted over the music

"Okay, special shout out to the West Orange High prom queen and birthday girl in VIP," The DJ said, pouring spotlights into VIP on Varshay and D'Shawn. *Oh my gosh!* She thought bashfully!

"Happy birthday, Varshay Lewis!!" the DJ retorted as the club exhilarated in ovation full of cheers and I love you Varshay's.

"Oh my gosh!" Varshay exclaimed, covering her mouth with her hands in complete astonishment. Out of nowhere, the bottles and a three-layer chocolate cake by the bartenders came, officially kicking off the party in VIP. Cameras were constantly flashing and Facebook had the couple of the night likes in the highs.

"Now this is how you bring eighteen in, bitch!" Yalunder shouted, bumping champagne glasses with Varshay filled to the rim of the coconut Cîroc.

"This is the best night of my life!!" screamed Varshay, hugging on to D'Shawn, letting the entire club know that he was her man, and the man in the entire club. *He is doin' it big for my birthday and he is not just talking, he's walking... unlike T-Mac,* Varshay thought. The special event for the West Orange High students at Club Maxwell was a Kodak moment itself. There were so many underage motha-fuckas getting drunk, despite not being able to purchase the alcohol themselves. *Damn, this is the best night of my life,* Varshay thought highlighting the precious night.

Sitting alone at the minibar in his suite, drinking straight from the bottle of Remy Martin, T-Mac had entrapped himself in a storm of dismal. It was Varshay's birthday, the day she could now say that she was a grown woman, and instead of enjoying the night with her, he had to watch another nigga bring a smile to her face. Watching the celebration on Facebook was heartbreaking.

The pain in his chest seem like a constant drum ready to explode through his flesh. Looking at his iPhone, T-Mac dried his tears that cascaded inevitably. If his homies saw how weak he was, he was certain that they would look at him as a soft-hearted ass nigga. But then again, they knew how much Varshay had meant to him. There was nothing to assuage the pain of loneliness but inebriation from the Remy Martin that was a swig left of a fifth.

How the fuck did I let this happen to me? I had the queen of Newark and like a precious lost diamond, she slipped from my hands. Just to be found by a nigga that stole cars for a livin'. Why? T-Mac thought then began to chuckle absentmindedly. He had no clue why he was laughing as it intensified to a demonical state. Unable to bridle his emotions, T-Mac erupted violently, throwing the Remy bottle against the concrete wall behind the counter of the minibar.

SMASH!

"I will kill you, bitch! You will not disrespect me, bitch!" T-Mac screamed out in rage, then broke down crying hysterically.

As both couples left the club, both Varshay and Yalunder were extremely intoxicated and very loquacious. D'Shawn and Tony, on the other hand, were ready to get to the Hilton Hotel and get their women in the opulent suites. They were just enjoying the night, not wanting it to end. Both women were ignoring their parents' concerned calls.

"Damn mom, what do she want?" Yalunder spoke sluggishly while trying to read the blurry text from her mom.

Tony P and D'Shawn tried their best to constrain their laughter, but didn't do a good job at it. In unison, they both erupted in laughter.

"What's so damn funny, y'all?" Varshay said with a smirk on her face. "Don't be picking on my friend, D'Shawn!" Varshay said punching D'Shawn in his arm softly.

"What? Now you want to beat me up. She the one over there sounding like she has a mouth full of fried chicken. Like some country ass woman!" D'Shawn exclaimed grabbing Varshay in a warming embrace.

"Whatever D'Shawn!" Yalunder said sluggishly giving D'Shawn the middle finger.

"It's okay baby, we got plenty ponies to ride on the country farm," Tony P said backing up his woman, simultaneously rubbing on her thighs, causing an electrifying wave of horniness to trigger her love box juices to flow.

Now he knows that's my sensitive spot, thought Yalunder crossing her legs. When she looked over at Varshay, she saw the awestruck look upon her face as she stared at the Hilton Hotel. On the front of the building, embellished in pretty pink and blue lights, was a message for Varshay. It read: "HAPPY BIRTHDAY VARSHAY LEWIS."

"Oh my gosh, D'Shawn!!" Varshay exclaimed in awe with tears in her eyes.

Wow! Yalunder thought in awe. *This man is the truth,* Varshay though as she attacked D'Shawn by jumping in his lap and kissing him deeply. She'd forgotten about Tony P and Yalunder, who were as well wrapped in each other's passionate smooching. When the chauffer opened the back doors, and saw the couples engaged in a smooching contest, he just shook his head, but deeply wished that he could be in both of the men's places at the moment. The two beautiful women looked like the two happiest women in the world.

"Welcome to Hilton Hotel," the chauffer spoke in a deep African accent.

━━━

She felt the A/C hit her face and did as D'Shawn requested and directed her to do. Then she heard the room door being closed, then locked.

"Two more steps, baby," D'Shawn said standing in front of Varshay, who walked towards him blindfolded.

"Okay, when I remove them, keep your eyes closed baby," said D'Shawn.

"Okay," Varshay spoke softly.

It's happening, I can't believe this, Varshay thought, she felt D'Shawn removing the blindfold from her eyes and caught a moment of his Polo cologne that lingered amongst him, and sent her mind to sexual overdrive. *No excuses tonight baby,* Varshay thought with a smile on her face.

"Okay, you can open them now," said D'Shawn, *here it goes!*

When Varshay opened her eyes, she was completely lost for words, staring at all the money scattered on the queen size bed and red and white rose petals everywhere on the floor. The room was illuminated by scented cinnamon candles with birthday balloons, red and white, tied to the bed.

Wow! she thought.

"I can't thank you enough, D'Shawn..."

"That's okay baby, I just want you to promise me something—"

"What is it, D'Shawn?" Varshay asked while walking towards D'Shawn, backing him up towards the bed until he was forced to sit down.

"Promise me that I won't have to kill no nigga about my woman, and that we will continue to work on growing into the extraordinary," said D'Shawn caressing Varshay's soft succulent ass with his hands up her dress, looking up into her eyes.

"I will, D'Shawn," Varshay said, pushing D'Shawn backwards on the bed and climbing on top of him.

"No excuses baby... remember!" Varshay said, stripping D'Shawn out of his suit, then wildly coming out of her dress. Slowly, they took their time with each other and made sweet, passionate love to each other on the pile of scattered money that summed to $50,000, all going to Varshay.

⸺

"Deeper daddy, deeper! Aww! Aww! Tony! Ooh!" Yalunder moaned out to the top of her lungs as Tony P rapidly entered her hairless, phat, excessively wet pussy. He had her in a missionary cannonball, grateful for her flexibility.

"Beat this pussy up, daddy... punish me, daddy!"

"You want this dick, baby!?" Screamed Tony P covered in sweat that dripped on Yalunder's sweaty face. He was going deeper with every thrust, hitting her g spot.

"Yes daddy! Yes!" She cried out in ecstasy.

Damn I hate to end this shit, I'mma miss her, Tony P thought as he aggressively pounded Yalunder's pussy.

"Em cumming, em cumming!!" Yalunder screamed. When Tony P saw her eyes fluttering and rolling to the back of her head, he knew that he was in overdrive.

"Arghhh!" Tony P groaned out as he came to his peak, exploding.

"Nooo!" Yalunder screamed when Tony P pulled out and shot his load all over her breasts and face. *I don't know why he always pullin' out. What's the sense of fuckin me raw if you ain't tryna man up?* She thought exhausted from the hardcore fucking.

Hours later, Yalunder laid in bed and thought seriously about her and Tony P. She loved him and wanted to have his kids, but was experiencing a new, unwelcoming reconsideration. She felt that she was alone and left behind in their fairy tale. *She could remember the times when he spoke highly of wanting her to bear his child. Something is going on for him to all of a sudden have a change of heart... and I will find out. Lord please reveal to me what's in the darkness that I cannot see but need to know,* Yalunder prayed silently in her head, then wiped the inevitable tears cascading down her face away. For the first time in their relationship, starting from the 9th grade, Yalunder felt unhappy, and wanted to venture with a man she just couldn't have. *Damn, temptation is a bitch!* she thought.

CHAPTER 13

"YES MAMA! Toya... Damn, that shit feels good!" Nicole moaned out as her girlfriend Latoya ate her pussy from the back. Nicole had her enormous succulent ass in the air and face buried in Latoya's silk pillows. Latoya was a beautiful big boned woman with a flawless caramel skin complexion. She was bisexual, and the girl to know in Camden, NJ. Latoya was a big player in the dope game and supplied 75% of Camden with the best quality of cocaine and heroin. Half of the niggas in Camden were employed by her and put their life on the line for her.

Nicole wasn't only her girlfriend, she was LaToya's right-hand girl, and their relationship was highly furtive. Latoya regulated Camden and had keys to every hustler's safe. The mansion she lived in would put a lot of rappers and Hollywood stars to shame. She only had one problem... Camden was in a drought on heroin. Her connect had backed out of the dope game with no warning, and left her with no food source to continue feeding Camden. Despite sending Nicole to try seducing him to supply them with one last shipment, he tenaciously remained adamant. Now they had to think of a plan to bring life back to Camden.

"Oh my gosh baby, I'm cumming!" Nicole purred as she came to an electrifying orgasm.

Latoya was there to catch her creamy load and slurped Nicole's cum up like a slushy. Nicole started resisting, trying to get away from Latoya sucking on her very sensitive clitoris.

"Girl, stop!" Nicole screamed pushing Latoya head away while laughing. "Girl, you play too much!" Nicole screamed after escaping Latoya's torturing, then running to the bathroom to refresh herself.

"Bitch, you stay running from this fire head!" Latoya screamed as Nicole looked herself in the bathroom. Since hooking up wit' Leon, Nicole had been getting some good fucking. Her nigga Bently got locked up, and all of his friends failed at trying to fuck her but one. *Latoya.*

She herself couldn't believe how their connect had left them out in the cold. *He claims that he is done with the game... but I know the truth. He feels that Bently's incarceration is a risk,* Nicole thought as the steaming hot water cascaded down her gorgeous, curvaceous body. *The heroin game was too sweet to just let it end like this... something got to give,* Nicole thought determinedly, thinking of one final suggestion. She just needed time to let her sources reveal to her the answers.

Latoya, as well, was in deep thought of trying to see how she was going to find a new heroin connect. She definitely wasn't about to buy no bap ass shit that came from New York. The junkies had informed all her dope holes in Camden to leave the bap shit in New York. The shit was like wet dope that couldn't sell, and had caused her a tremendous loss, because she invested largely. *I can't believe dis pussy ass third world country motherfucka just turned cold feet on me,* Latoya thought as she laid on her side and rocked her lower body rhythmically, something she did out of habit, and used as a meditation tool. When the bathroom door opened up, and Nicole walked out with nothing on, Latoya wanted to go for round three. Nicole could tell just by the lustful look in Latoya's eyes, what was the predominately on Latoya's mind at the moment.

"We need to make an offer that he can't refuse," said Latoya.

"And what's that?" Nicole retorted, sliding into a black satin thong and bra.

"Bring pressure to him and make him give us the source. We've been too faithful to him to let him do us any kind of way," Latoya said. What she was saying made sense and Nicole was always down with her bitch.

Up until Bentley got popped with a couple ounces and sentenced to twelve years, shit was good. He took his time like a man, and if that bitch think that we will bring heat to him, then he has already sabotaged in his perspectives, Nicole thought, as she slid into a pair of white PZI jeans, and a black blouse.

"Toya, I'mma be back in the morning. But while I'm gone, I will be seeing what's up."

"Where you going that you can't make it back home to me tonight, bitch?" Latoya asked half-joking.

"Bitch, I'm going to see Leon, I need him to beat my back out," said Nicole spraying herself down with Riri perfume.

"So' when you goin' to let me sample him?" Latoya asked, badly wanting a threesome with Nicole and a man. But she knew that Nicole was too abashed, and very furtive about her sexuality indifferences. And Latoya was the only one Nicole trusted with her secret.

"Never bitch, over my drunk body," Nicole retorted, popping a molly in her mouth, then washing it down with Latoya's glass of punch juice.

"Give me kiss," said Nicole, leaning into Latoya's sexy lips. They kissed each other slow, and passionate.

"I love you."

"I love you too," Nicole retorted, then departed from the mansion with Leon on her mind and on speed dial. Nicole wanted to surprise Leon, so instead of hopping into her pink Range Rover, she pulled out in her turbo toy, a cherry red Ferrari 360 spider.

"Now, that's how a bad bitch ride!" Nicole exclaimed as she accelerated, burning rubber, from the mansion.

Their two days at the Hilton Hotel were a complete love rollercoaster for D'Shawn and Varshay. From sun up to sun down they were saturated into each other's bodily fluids. It was heaven to Varshay. *It's amazing what beauty can afford you in life,* she thought as she sat on D'Shawn's lap in the jacuzzi in their hotel suite. Yalunder and Tony P had left two days ago, being that their suite was only reserved for one night. With her arms laced around his neck and a glass of champagne in her hands, she took in D'Shawn's handsomeness. He'd given her $50,000 in cash, and $30,000 on a debit card. At eighteen years old, she wouldn't ever in a million years thought that it would turn out like this. Nor did she even see T-Mac coming out his pockets that deep. It was an enigma of how she felt for him deep down, ineffably. And it frustrated her at times, but she did know that she cared for him and didn't want to lose him.

"What's going through that big head of yours?" D'Shawn said to Varshay caught up in her thoughts. They were both naked, enjoying the nudity of each other, and the opportunity to explore each other. She knew every mark on his body and he knew hers. *Something that T-Mac can't detail,* she thought. Varshay emptied her glass and set it on the edge of the jacuzzi, then looked in D'Shawn's anticipating eyes. *He always gives me his undivided attention,* she observed, kissing him softly on his lips with her arms around his neck.

"So that's what you're thinking 'bout?"

"Shut up, boy!" Varshay said laughing at his hilarious character.

"Graduation is next week baby," Varshay said.

"So, what are your plans?" D'Shawn asked

"Umm..." She guessed in complete indecisiveness. "Nothing too spectacular..." She retorted nonchalantly

"What you mean...you gotta go to college!!"

"Did you go?" Varshay spat with an attitude that D'Shawn quickly picked up on. He gave her an ugly look that turned her on, despite knowing that she'd made him upset.

"Nawl I ain't go to college, and I never got a chance to graduate."

"Baby, I didn't mean to sound judgmental," Varshay said, attempting to soothe the sudden mood change in the atmosphere. "Baby, I'm sorry," she purred kissing his lips gently, simultaneously caressing his face.

"I'm okay baby, and whatever you choose to do, I got your back," D'Shawn said caressing Varshay's beautiful face while staring in her eyes. He sensed an emotional transformation from the look in her eyes.

"That's sweet D'Shawn and I will always have your back too, boo!" Varshay retorted. "I was thinking real estate agency."

"That's a start. Do you have the knowledge or is that just a random picking?" D'Shawn asked.

"Random," Varshay retorted. Despite her father's expectations of wanting to see her go to school for Criminology to become a prosecutor, she just couldn't deal with all the hours that it would take her away from D'Shawn. Something that she would never tell him, especially after just seeing how serious he took her future planning. She'd never hear the end of it.

"Whatever, whenever, I will back you. One day, I plan to step away from this game a business man, and I will," D'Shawn said determinedly.

"I don't want to lose you, or for you to go anywhere," Varshay said, then began kissing on D'Shawn's bottom lip passionately.

D'Shawn lifted Varshay and sat her on the edge of the jacuzzi. She wrapped both of her legs around him as he kissed her down to her breasts, and without favoritism, sucked on both erected nipples. Her moans intensified.

The flawlessness of her delicate yellow skin amazed him as it glistered from the water. D'Shawn grabbed both of Varshay's legs and put them on each of his shoulders. When he entered Varshay's sultry, phat juicy mound with his enormous sized dick. She arched her back and purred loudly and ecstatically.

"Awww! D'Shawn!"

He slow stroked her rhythmically as she sat back on her hands, gyrating her hips in synchronization to the rhythm of his thrusting in and out her excessively wet pussy.

"Daddy! Awww! Uhh! Uhhh!" She moaned out, feeling D'Shawn's throbbing penis continue to grow deeper, hitting her g-spot with every single stroke. He pounded her tight pussy for half an hour before she came to a third orgasm.

"Emm cumin again, D'Shawn! She shouted with trembling legs. He felt himself about to explode and reached in to kiss her. She felt him on the verge as well, and wrapped her legs tightly.

CHAPTER 14

As LEE COASTED on I-95 in the black Suburban, he was relieved to
see the sign: Entering Palm Beach County. He'd been on the road
since sun up, only stopping three times to fully fuel up. The DMX
emanating from his speakers made him want to take hustling to
another level. Skip had sent him on his second trip to Florida dolo in
two weeks to drop off five kilos of heroin to power house clientele. It
was a risk, but Lee knew the procedure well. As long as he drove at a
normal speed then there was nothing to worry about. He enjoyed the
scenery of Florida palm trees and the beautiful women.

*This nigga Skip reach is way in Florida. Shit, that's the entire East
Coast,* Lee thought, as the Migos lyrics emanated from the SUV
speakers. When Lee got to the mile warning sign for the Lakeworth
exit, he maneuvered over to the right lane. A couple seconds later he
got off at the Lakeworth exit. Out of nowhere, a troubling revelation
came to him.

*We getting money, we making plays, when will we get to get to
this status. Does Skip have lessons to teach us how to get to where he
is? How the fuck we a team? Shit, we done paid him enough money to
pay for the game he gave us,* Lee thought. *Where does the elevation
come in at?* Lee wanted to know.

It was something vague that had him bothersome, he felt that him and his clique were obliging too much accommodation to Skip. He was now skeptical of the prospect of other niggas paying a percentage of what they made. Then, on the other hand, didn't want to feel as if he was developing any type of jealousy against Skip, not know that the fact of his skeptical thoughts was closer than dawn. When Lee pulled up to McDonald's parking lot shortly off the exit, he parked and waited for the blue Benz truck to pull up next to him, before he activated the secret compartment in the dashboard where the heroin was safely stored. When the black man who favored Vince Young stepped out his truck, Lee unlocked the door and allowed him to hop inside the passenger side. The Vince Young lookalike entered the Suburban with a black Nike duffel bag. Like last time, he looked down at the mac-10 on Lee's lap, and hurried on with the transaction. He opened the duffel bag and showed Lee that all the money was there.

"Listen, it's all there man, but I need something else that slipped my mind," the man said, scratching the back of his head nervously. "I knew that you were already on the road. So, I decided to send the message back with you."

"So what's on ya mind, B?" Lee asked in his Jersey accent while pulling the five kilos of heroin out the secret stash compartment and placing them inside another black Nike empty duffel bag, moving quickly.

"Well, I know he charge 18.5 for a key up there and he want to make—"

"What did you just say?... 18.5 for a key of what?" Lee asked with an ominous look upon his face, frightening this man.

"18.5 for a key of cocaine, homie. But down here we sell them at 30 apiece." *And we bought them 35 a piece,* Lee thought fretfully.

"Has he ever did 18.5 fo' you?" Lee asked probing the man.

"On two occasions, and that's what I'm lookin' fo' now. Did he go up on the prices?" The man asked skeptically.

When he searched Lee's face he knew that something was wrong.

Lee locked the doors quickly aimed the mac-10 in the dude's frightened face.

"Call that nigga and let him know that you want to put in an order fo' the next trip and want know will 18.5 still be on the table... or better yet B, you just tell him you have 18.5," Lee directed the scary man to do, while he accessed his recording device on his iPhone with his free hand.

"Okay man," the man said tremulously, afraid of what could happen and more daunted by not knowing what could happen. He had no clue of what was going on... he was completely perplexed.

"This not with you B, just do as I say and there should be no problems," Lee retorted, attempting to assuage the man's level of panic.

"Thank God man, I thought it was me," the man said, then did as he was told, and put the iPhone on speaker phone without Lee telling him to do so. The iPhone rung three times before Skip's distinctive voice emanated from the phone.

"What's good with the sunshine?" Skip asked, already knowing who the caller was, saved as Florida in his phone contacts.

"Hey umm, your guy ain't roll up on me yet. I know that he's far out of your reach, but that's okay. Listen man, in two days I'mma need a bar of that white girl product—"

"How many you talkin', Poppa, you already know that you good," said Skip, ready to do numbers with his clientele.

"I'm goin' to need ten flat, Skip," Poppa retorted.

"That's good. Since it's 18.5, just give me 18 flat for good business... I love yo' money," Skip complimented.

"That's good lookin', Skip," Poppa said sweating excessively.

"Okay, when my man make it back, I'mma load him up and send him back your way in two days," said Skip.

"Okay, that's cool... Bet that up Skip. I really appreciate you, dawg," said Poppa.

"No, I appreciate you," said Skip, then disconnected the call.

Poppa took a long sigh and then spoke, "It's done man, I did what you told me."

"How much you really tryin' to get?" Lee asked still pointing the mac-10 in Poppa's face.

———

"Two seconds nigga, please," Leon retorted. They were in the living room playing Madden 2016 on the sixty-four-inch flat screen TV.

"D'Shawn, come help us!" Varshay screamed from the kitchen.

"Okay, one second!" D'Shawn retorted, agitated because Leon had got the football deep in his red zone promising to score.

"Two seconds with one play," Leon whistled. "By it's not lookin' good," Leon said, provocatively trying to fluctuate the momentum of the game. He knew that talking shit would get under D'Shawn's skin.

"Yeah whatever, fat boy," D'Shawn exclaimed feigned worry.

"There he goes! Larry Fitzgerald!" Leon shouted as he sent a touchdown pass into the end zone for a touchdown.

"Nigga that's luck, B!" D'Shawn said, throwing down the game controller to the PS3, and giving Leon $100 for his loss bet.

The only two people missing in the immediate family was Lee and Grandma Patty. When D'Shawn had pulled up to the ruined, creature-infested rowhouse in the U-Haul truck and told everyone to get to packing. Grandma Patty down the road declined to move out of the roach and rat-infested building. Instead of wanting a new environment, she wanted to die in all that she knew. When he thought about it from a narrower perspective, he was experiencing the same precariousness of not wanting to let go of the streets. He was complacent to the street life. *I could be a pro boxer right now. Instead, I choose to live in the streets. One day I will let them go... just not right now,* D'Shawn thought as he walked into the kitchen to help his mom and Varshay out.

"Okay, what can I do for you ladies?"

Seeing his mom and Varshay getting along gave him a warming

comfort. He was feeling Varshay and saw himself falling for what he was afraid to embrace. Not knowing that it had already taken its course on its own development. D'Shawn never experiencing it with any other female, could not deny the fact the he was in... love, like never before.

———

"Yo, I'mma need twenty of them Ms. Becky's favorite. When can I pick them up?" Skip asked his connect over the phone.

"How about tomorrow, you come in to see me so we could discuss this."

"Is there a problem?" Skip retorted skeptically, sensing something amiss.

"No, no, no there's no problem. It's just something that I need to run by you," responded Skip's connect.

"Okay I'll be there," Skip retorted.

"Okay and we'll handle business," Skip connect retorted then disconnected the call

What the fuck he got to tell me other than getting this money? These third world country mothafuckas be spooking me out fo' real, Skip thought to himself.

He was in his Range Rover on his way to pick up a girl named, Celeste to take her out on a romantic dinner. She was originally from Harlem and had no clue of the category of hurricane coming in her direction. Nor did Skip know himself, that he was the category four hurricane.

When Skip pulled up to Celeste's residence in West Orange, NJ, she sashayed out her home she shared with her sister Tamara. He watched her sexy undulations come towards him, awestruck at her beauty.

"Damn this bitch bad," Skip exclaimed while looking at Celeste in her black Prada catsuit and rich bear fur coat, and heels.

"Hi Skip, where we going, baby?" Celeste asked Skip when she stepped into the Range Rover.

"It's a surprise... so enjoy the ride, pretty," Skip retorted, turning up the volume to his Tank hit.

━━━

E-Money had the junkies out of control coming from a long distant across Camden just to get the good heroin. He was on 123rd in Camden projects locking it down thoroughly. He'd sold eighteen ounces, double its original price, and three quarters for triple its original price. If niggas wanted to hustle, then he was going to make them pay for the product. He respected the drought, not the niggas who wanted to come up. It was only temporary for him, and the profit was his only concern.

"Yo nephew, let me get a gram of that boy," a junkie said, walking up on E-Money who sat on the stairs to a project building.

"Do you have what it takes for a gram, Unc?" E-Money asked the old man, who was sprung out on heroin.

"$200 nephew, straight... now let me get a nice one!" The old man said. When he handed the money over to E-Money, a gunshot exploded the old man's head.

Boom! Clink! Clink! The old man blood and brains splattered on E-Money's face. When the old man fell on the stairs next to E-Money, he saw two big niggas with two Mossberg's aimed at his face. He was an assassin himself, but even assassins knew better than to resist a jack move.

"What? You niggas won't to rob me, huh?" E-Money asked, undaunted by the two niggas that had his life in their hands at the pull of a trigga, and wore ski masks on their faces.

"Nawl, but somebody want to see you, and you have no other choice but to come, or else you'll be joining that old man," said the big man to the left of him

"Who want me?" E-Money asked.

"Mama Toya, nigga," the big man on the right of him retorted smiling, revealing a top and bottom gold grill in his mouth.

On the ride to Toya's mansion, E-Money's mind was in all directions vagrantly, not knowing whether or not he was taking his last ride or another job assignment. Latoya ran the streets of Camden, and if it was because he had what she lacked, then that meant being dead or tortured wouldn't be a prudent move. And before he gave her anything he would have to get paid himself. He'd just learned himself that Skip dealt with heroin, and only a few people could take you straight to Skip. Those who couldn't do that were the ones who would never know that Skip was the actual lifeline to the heroin. What had E-Money perplexed was Skip's overlooking Camden's drought to come shut it down himself, or with Latoya.

Something just didn't sit right with that picture. *Shit, a hustler will get it by any means,* E-Money thought as the black Lincoln town car accelerated to Latoya's mansion.

CHAPTER 15

"MAN, THIS NIGGA BEEN PLAYIN' us, B," Lee screamed frantically to D'Shawn and Leon outside their trap house on 129th and Kentucky.

As soon as Lee made it into Jersey, he'd called D'Shawn and Leon and told them to assemble at the trap. They sensed the amiss and strapped up with their AK47s ready for whatever Lee had to tell them. But being ready and being prepared didn't sit in comparison with the bombshell that he'd just dropped on them.

It was unfathomable to D'Shawn until he'd listened to the recording of Skip and his clientele's conversation.

"18.5 and this nigga was killin' us, breakin' our necks for 35 flat, B!" Exclaimed Lee.

"I can't believe this nigga," said Leon.

D'Shawn sat quiet in a vengeance state of mind. He was troubled of how Skip had manipulated him and his cousins. But the torment came from knowing the fact that he still knew nothing of the grimy game, especially if he was manipulated.

"Why the fuck we just sitting here talkin' 'bout how fucked up he did us and not goin' over there to fix this nigga?!" D'Shawn spat, sitting at the table with a nefarious look upon his face. And both Lee and Leon knew that it was the look of death. The trio knew what had to be done with no second considerations.

"Shit, let's go then," Leon retorted, cocking back his Mossberg 500. The trio left out the door to carry out a feasible mission. They felt betrayed in the worst way, and were out to deliver a "coup de grace" to the man that had deceived them all.

<hr>

"Listen, I haven't told you the reason why I'm holdin' off on Camden. If they somehow get a connect from someone else, then let it be theirs and not our product. I don't trust Bently and will not take the risk by feeding his fish," Skip's connect explained to him.

They were in a buffet booth in an Italian restaurant in West Orange, NJ. It was evident that his connect wanted no dealings with Camden, because of a close acquaintance with his connect's clientele had got knocked off. It wasn't until he'd thought about giving E-Money the kilo of heroin he understood the purpose of the meeting.

"Don't fault yourself for what you had no control of knowing, Skip. But my sources tell me that my heroin is floatin' in Camden as we speak. And the only way that'll be possible is—"

"If it came from me, which it did and if I would've known what you just told me then I t would of never happen," Skip said.

"Don't worry yourself Skip, let's just make sure from here on out, that we have no more misconceptions," Skip's connect forewarned him, then took a sip of his water. "We are understood, correct?"

"Yeah, we understood," Skip retorted.

"Okay, well come this afternoon to the Holiday Inn hotel on 26th and Collee," Skip's connect said, then buried his face in a plate of spaghetti, saying no more as he dismissed Skip with a booting hand gesture.

When Skip pulled up to his crib he saw that D'Shawn's BMW was in his driveway. He knew it was D'Shawn's car by the distinctive black rims. He was expecting Lee, but not D'Shawn.

Maybe Lee is driving D'Shawn's car, Skip thought as he emerged from the Range Rover. He knew that Celeste would probably still be asleep. But then again, she had to get up to open the door for Lee. *But, the bitch ain't answer the phone when I tried callin' either,* Skip thought.

When he put his key into the door, he heard moans to no misconceptions.

What the fuck... I know this hoe ain't fucking another nigga in my shit! Skip thought as he came into the house ready to check the slut bitch. Skip froze in his tracks like a deer caught in headlights and stared in bewilderment at the tremendous wreck of vandalism of his home. Instinctively, Skip pulled out his Glock .19 from his waist and followed the intensifying sounds of Celeste's moans, absentmindedly. Every step of the way up the stairs, her moans of pleasure intensified.

"Uhh! Uhh! Yess, daddy! Yess! Fuck me!"

I can't believe this dog ass slut! Skip thought angrily as he came to the edge of the stairs.

When Skip entered his room, he saw that it was completely dark. When he flicked on the light, he saw D'Shawn holding a gun to Celeste's head, and her shouting to her lungs in feigned moans. Shit became incoherent in Skip's mind.

"What the fuck, B!" Skip screamed, not understanding why D'Shawn had his bitch held up at gunpoint.

"Shut up, bitch!" D'Shawn screamed to Celeste, who immediately ceased her feigned moans with a stream of tears cascading down her face.

"So tell me Skip, what have I ever done to you for you to cheat me out of the game, B?"

"What the fuck you talkin' 'bout, nigga!?" Skip screamed in rage, pointing the Glock .19 at D'Shawn's head. *Kill the nigga!* Skip's instincts told him.

"You know exactly what I'm talking 'bout. So, 18.5 is what you givin' a kilo up fo' right, and makin me pay 35 flat to you. Damn Skip, I thought we were a team man!" D'Shawn expressed himself with an ominous look upon his face.

"Nigga, every duck got to learn how to swim on their own. What makes you different, nigga?" Skip said, ready to pull the trigger.

"What makes me different is that I'mma live and you not, bitch ass nigga."

BAM! Out from behind, after creeping up on him swiftly, Lee smashed Skip in the back of his head with the butt end of his Mossberg pump, knocking Skip's lights completely out.

"Pussy nigga," Lee expressed.

"Let's get this nigga to the basement, her too," Leon said.

"No please don't hurt me. I have not—"

BAM!

"Bitch shut up!" D'Shawn said as he slammed his Glock .50 into Celeste's temple knocking her unconscious along with Skip.

The treatment that E-Money was getting at the mansion as a hostage was first class paradise. Since arriving at the luxurious mansion, E-Money had been isolated in a section of the mansion that could serve as a small efficiency. He had no connection with the outside world communication-wise. But he did enjoy the two Cuban bisexuals who pleased him beyond extravagant necessities. He'd been bound to the small efficiency for one day now. And times, he would think that she would come work him into exhaustion, then come take him out. Because he had no clue what the queen of Camden had in mind, nor when he would see her. But then the logical interference would flash before him. *A dead man is no good fo' her,* E-Money thought while getting his dick sucked in bed with the Cuban women. While one sucked his dick, the other ate her friend's pussy.

If this is how a playa went to the grave then I guess this is what they call paradise, E-Money thought enjoying the sweet fellation to his dick. Outside his door were two armed bodyguards, and he hadn't yet to come up with a plan to get past his ossification.

———

When T-Mac caught wind to D'Shawn's distribution of heroin, he became furious and saw that as crossing the line. He'd bridled himself for bringing wrath directly to D'Shawn, and anyone who was affiliated with him, to avoid any misconception of a motive. He refused to have people insinuate that the beef was behind D'Shawn fucking Varshay. T-Mac and Bean were riding through D'Shawn's turf looking for a random individual that would fit the criterion, to execute the task that needed to be accomplished.

"Yo blood, that's Radio right there. He'll be perfect, plus that's my unc," said Bean, from the passenger side of T-Mac's BMW truck.

"Well we goin' to see," T-Mac retorted, pulling up to the Arab corner store on 123rd and Boston, letting down his window.

"Yo Radio, check it out!" T-Mac called out to Radio who was sitting on a black crate amongst fiends in oily clothes. Folks called him Radio because he walked around beat bopping all day long.

And could drop a beat for a free style competitive like no other. When T-Mac called him he smiled, revealing his rotten grill. On his way to the car, he busted out with an old school beat bop. T-Mac and Bean bobbed their heads rhythmically to the funky beat, which enticed Radio to do a funky dance along with the beat. Radio was cutting a fool like he was in the 70's again.

"Oh shit, Radio!" T-Mac said in enthusiasm as Radio crisscrossed his legs like Michael Jackson, increasing the ruination of his talking Converse sneakers.

"Okay, okay Radio, check it out Unc. I need you to handle some for me," T-Mac said, displaying a capsule of heroin that got Radio's full attention.

"What, what, what that, that fo' nephew?!" Radio stuttered with his eyes wide open in a trance between him and the capsule.

"C'mere Unc," Bean said when Radio reached for the capsule, T-Mac pulled back quickly.

"No junkie stunts, now... I need you to get me a gram from whoever got this on the street."

"I, I know, know, know who got it," Radio said stuttering.

"Okay then, go get me a gram... run off with my money and you better keep runnin' until you're out of Jersey. Because when I find you, I will kill you!" T-Mac said handing Radio $75 to go purchase a gram.

"We 'bout to see what these niggas hittin' on, B!" said T-Mac as he watched Radio walk down the street then turn into an alley.

Twenty minutes had passed, and they saw Radio emerged from the ally strutting towards them with his fist balled up and a big smile on his face gladsomely taking long strides.

"If he don't look like a happy hour I'm a fool," said T-Mac.

"Okay nephew, I got the, the gram." Radio stuttered as he handed T-Mac less than a gram.

"Unc, this the whole gram?" T-Mac asked skeptically, already knowing from the looks of it that it wasn't.

"Yeah, nephew!" Radio screamed feeling insulted by his integrity. T-Mac looked at the heroin and compared the looks to his heroin.

"They could only be getting this from one person!" T-Mac said looking Bean in his eyes. His enemy having the same product he had, only told him that they had the same connect, which definitely meant war. *That's why they call it drug wars,* T-Mac thought committed to his next move.

"Bean, it's time to wash these niggas!" Said T-Mac.

"Damn right Blood, blatt!" Exclaimed Bean,

"Soo woo!" T-Mac Blood called to Bean.

They left Radio a happy junkie with the gram and their own

capsule. When they were gone up the street and vanished from sight, Radio combined the less than a gram with what he'd pocketed from the gram.

"Aye Radio, you goin' to get me high and get some of this good pussy?" A trick named Carla asked Radio who had full blown AIDS.

"Yeah, yeah, yeahhh!" Radio stuttered. He was excited to be able to pay for a piece of ass despite knowing, like everyone else, that Carla had AIDS. Together they had walked gladsomely to an abandoned rowhouse to satisfy each other.

CHAPTER 16

WHEN SKIP HAD FINALLY COME AROUND to a blurry conscious with a throbbing headache, He immediately realized that he was bound to a chair and in a perilous situation. He was in his basement and defenseless against his enemies. When he turned his head to the side, he immediately vomited at the gruesome deformity of Celeste's face. Apparently, she was still breathing, which was evident from the sound of snorting that came from her nose's nasal wall and passage. *They cut off her nose,* Skip thought refusing to look at her again. He felt bad for how she'd got caught up in his beef, and knew that it was too late to save her, or himself. *Damn, how the fuck didn't I see this shit comin'?* Skip thought to himself afraid.

When he heard the door open up then feet descending the stairs, he braced himself to face his enemies. When the individual stepped in front of him, Skip was deeply perplexed, as he stared his connect in his eyes.

"From what I'm hearing, it doesn't please me at all."

"What the fuck is this? I thought we were down, Bobby!" Skip screamed in a raging fit.

"That's what I thought too, Skip, but apparently you feel the need to fuck over a good friend of mine, then you continue to do business with the Florida boy that I seriously warned you about," said Bobby in his Arab accent. *Man, I'm dead. This man is not a man to screw over, and for him to know what he knows means that he has my phone,* Skip thought, unable to give Bobby any bogus excuse. There wasn't an excuse in the world to explain his infidelity to the man who had him on top of Jersey, and the East Coast by himself.

SMACK! Bobby vigorously slapped Skip with a powerful backhand.

"What do you have to say for yourself, huh?" Bobby screamed while pulling out a Colt Python .375 and aiming at Celeste.

BOOM! BOOM!

The shots exploded Celeste's face, causing more deformity, and killing her instantly. The loud shots had put Skip into a tremulous state, and caused him to shit his pants.

"I trusted you, and gave you the world. You never know whom my friends are, and you never are supposed to forget who you are," Bobby spat lifting Skip's chin up with the tip of the .357.

"I'mma give you a chance Skip, only one chance, and tell me where is the rest of the product, huh?" Bobby asked, looking in Skip's daunted eyes. Skip swallowed his fear and spoke.

"The gamble house on 151st and Spruce. My boy Borack knows where to find it," Skip said, displeasing Bobby and making him more delirious at how easy he was to capitulate under pressure.

"You disappoint me Skip, I would've lost my money if I would've bet my money that you were a strong man. I would had lost my money!" Bobby shouted, then jammed the .357 in Skip's mouth and pulled the trigger.

BOOM! BOOM!

"Dead men can't talk or disobey," Bobby said to Skip's lifeless body, then made his exit of the palace.

━━━

When Lee had received the call from Bobby and got the information needed to find the kilos of heroin that Skip had stashed, he was on his way and had D'Shawn and his brother to back him. They were working to build a consolidation with Bobby and to show him that they had what it took to replace Skip. After searching Skip's cell phone thoroughly, Lee stumbled across the familiar number that was Bobby's. He began to probe once seeing that Bobby was saved in his phone as "Boy connect." When Lee had called Bobby, he got straight to the point and asked Bobby how much of Skip's life that he needed. When Bobby had caught on to the situation and caller, all that was left was to hear his friend out. For a while, Bobby wanted to introduce the dope game to Lee and elevate him from stealing cars. If he'd known that Skip was cheating Lee out his money, he would've immediately cut Skip off. Bobby became angry and knew what he had to do, and refused to let Lee or anyone in his crew do his job.

"When Bobby told you to cut a person off they had best do what he say," were the words Bobby told Lee. They had no more worries, because after tonight, Bobby would teach them the correct fundamentals of the dope game. When Lee, D'Shawn, and Leon pulled up to the gambling house in East Orange on 151st and Spruce, they observed of how isolated the block was. It was daylight and they were taking risk with the ardent sun. But like every high crime neighborhood in New Jersey, there was no one specific time to add onto the murder rate. Furthermore, school was in session and wouldn't be into cessation until after Lee and his crew were gone.

"I'mma go inside, when I stick my head out, Lee come in. Leon keep your eyes and ears open and us on speed dial," D'Shawn directed.

"Let's do this," Leon exclaimed.

They all were eager to be getting the job done, so that they could be down with the main man, Bobby.

Dressed in all-black with a skully on his head, D'Shawn emerged from the Suburban and knocked on the door to the gambling house.

"Who is it?" An older man's husky voice asked.

"Dee, Skip sent me," D'Shawn retorted. He heard the door being unlocked and stepped to the side so that the door could open outwards.

"Come in youngin'," the old school said, letting D'Shawn step inside the alcove. Once inside, he locked the door again.

"So what's up?" He asked D'Shawn.

"Skip sent me fo' Borack," D'Shawn answered.

"The only Borack Skip could be talkin' 'bout is me.," Borack exclaimed. Going with his gut instinct, D'Shawn took what the man said to be veridical.

"Skip sent me to have you put something up fo' him," D'Shawn said.

"Like what, youngin?" Borack retorted skeptically knowing how furtive Skip was, so seeing the young cat in his home talking about put something up was something unusual.

"Three kilos of that Boy," D'Shawn said,

"Tell Skip I don't know what he talkin' 'bout," Borack retorted. *Skip must be out his mind,* Borack thought.

So he going to play hardball, huh, thought D'Shawn.

"Okay, I'll tell him that," D'Shawn said, walking towards the door to leave.

"Wait, where is it?" Borack asked stopping D'Shawn.

"Yo Borack, do you want us to deal around you!" A man from the kitchen area screamed.

"Yeah, I have to handle something," Borack screamed back to his partner at the poker table.

"You got two minutes to go get it, 'cause I know that you don't got em on you."

"It's outside," D'Shawn fired back.

"Go get it," Borack retorted.

"It's coming to us," D'Shawn retorted as he opened the door and signaled for Lee to come inside with the duffel bag. When Lee made it to the door, and stepped inside the alcove with the duffel bag, all at once, him and D'Shawn pulled out their Glock. 21s and aimed them in Borack's face.

"One time only... who all in there?" D'Shawn asked. Borack was from the old school, and knew better than to resist a jack move. Especially to those who didn't come in shooting first. Them was the ones that only had one objective, and that was to get what came to get and go.

"Man, it's five of us," Borack said calmly.

"Where is the stash?" Asked D'Shawn.

"Man, I don't know what—"

BAM! Before he could utter the common lie, D'Shawn struck him in the mouth with his Glock, knocking out his four front teeth.

"Oh shit, aww!" Borack screamed out in pain.

"Yo Borack you—"

BOOM! BOOM! BOOM!

The loud screaming, and the sound of Borack falling to the floor caused the men at the table to run to his aid. D'Shawn whacked two of them while Lee killed off the last two of the four.

"Now we could do this the easy way or the hard way, Borack," said Lee pointing his smoking gun at Borack

"Man fuck you, young fuck nigga!" Borack screamed, holding his swollen bloody mouth.

"Fuck nigga, aye?" Lee retorted, kicking Borack in his mouth with his black Timberland boots.

"Arghhh!" Borack groaned out in pain.

"The easy way or the hard way, Borack," D'Shawn spat, trying his luck too adamantly for Borack.

"He! He! He! He! He!" Borack did the strangest thing that anyone would ever expect to do, and began laughing hysterically.

What the fuck he on, dog food? thought D'Shawn realizing that what seemed feasible turned out to be formidable.

"Champ, we got until I take my last breath," said Borack, spitting glob of blood from his mouth to the floor. *Damn!* D'Shawn thought. Then put out on a set of leather black gloves. It didn't matter how much they'd beaten Borack, he was an old school who lived by strict code and principle. "Never fold if not on the poker table." Together meticulously and thoroughly, they rampaged the entire house to the best of their ability trying to find the stash, to no avail.

"Man, this nigga ain't giving!" Lee screamed.

"Bitch ass nigga where is it, huh!" *Bam! Bam!*

Lee had finally lost it and began repeatedly smashing his Glock .21 into the face of Borack, pistol whipping him to death. The more gruesome the scene got, the deeper D'Shawn realized that he was in the game: knee deep. With nothing left to do he called Bobby.

"What's good, Dee?"

"Man, this nigga ain't sellin' his soul," D'Shawn retorted.

"What's left of him?" Bobby asked.

"Sure not his face, and a lot of blood."

"Did y'all turn any pillows?"

"We turned up the entire house," D'Shawn retorted

"Well Dee, it's there but not every man would sell their soul... them are the good ones. And it's something that you can't change nor be mad 'bout. Get out of there and the three of y'all come over to the shop," Bobby said then hung up.

"Let's go Lee," D'Shawn said, tucking the throw away phone away.

BOOM! BOOM!

D'Shawn put two slugs into Borack's face before leaving.

"He's already dead," Lee retorted laughing.

"So that's for all the hard time he gave," D'Shawn said.

All three of them left the chilling scene and headed over to the chop shop, where it all began for the trio.

"Now I see why he stayed at the gambling house," Lee said.

"Yeah, too bad we'll never find the stash," D'Shawn retorted.

"That nigga was a real nigga, he took his loyalty for Skip to his last breath."

"That's how I will die also, if ever put in the same situation," Lee retorted.

"He was no enemy and it wasn't personal. I say that we all give a toast to him," said D'Shawn.

"I say we all put our money together and open up a club called Club Borack," Leon said as he drove the Suburban gingerly.

"Hell yeah, B!" D'Shawn agreed.

"I got a feeling that we are 'bout to lock Newark and the East Coast down, B," Leon said as he came to a red light.

"I say that I got the same feeling as you, B," said D'Shawn.

"Me too," Lee retorted.

It was amazing how everything seemed to come back full circle. *Had I known what Skip was up to, I would have had his head like we do back in my country. Now that I have Lee's attention again... I could surely use him for what I have in store for Camden,* Bobby thought to himself sitting at his desk while getting his dick sucked by one of his gorgeous brunettes. He was ready, eagerly, to put his new team on the map.

CHAPTER 17

THE BODYGUARDS that guarded E-Money's door an hour ago had dropped him off a tailored Armani suit that fit him perfectly. Both of the Cuban women had been removed, which only showed E-Money that Latoya was ready to see him. When he was done, he sat on the leather sofa and waited, admiring the costly suit and shoes that made him feel like the man of Camden and a professional assassin. His mind was already made up on what he would do to undermine his captors. His life was not worth a profession that he didn't desire. He was a hitman, not a dope boy. When he heard the door unlocking, his stomach swarmed with butterflies. The black ass six-foot-five, 300lb bodyguard stepped inside, then waved E-Money over.

"Come on, she's waiting," the bodyguard said in a resounding voice. He had an earpiece in his ear, mumbling into his Bluetooth. "We're on our way from the east platform to the dining."

When E-Money and the bodyguard appeared in the dining room, the sounds of Fantasia emanated from a surround system hidden within the walls. At a set table under a crystal chandelier sat Latoya, sipping on a glass of Ace of Spades champagne. Cinnamon candles illuminated a romantic scenery. *Damn, she's beautiful,* E-Money thought as he came closer into her view. She had on a gorgeous

Alexander McQueen dress and heels the color of serpentine, with costly pearls from her ears to her wrist. The bodyguard pulled the seat out for E-Money and allowed him to take a seat closet to Latoya.

"Thanks Leroy," she said to the bodyguard who nodded his head in gratification then left the twosome alone. Her Pulse perfume redolently lingered among them. He'd only seen Latoya a couple times, but it was ever as close as he was now. The rumors of her scintillating beauty confirmed to be true. Latoya filled the empty glass in front of E-Money with a hypnotizable smile.

"How are you, E-Money?" Latoya asked in a very seducing voice that made E-Money's dick jump. *Shit, you should of came instead of the Cuban bitches. All that good meat on your bones, a nigga would never get enough,* E-Money so badly wanted to say but cleared his throat and spoke.

"I'm doing great...it's a pleasure to meet you, despite of the circumstances."

"Please don't be bothered E-Money, there are no hard feelings nor any beef," Latoya explained trying her best to soothe any discomfort that she may have caused E-Money.

"Don't worry ma—"

"Dinner, Latoya," a beautiful brunette scullion appeared in a black bikini with two plates of steaming lasagna.

As she set the plates down on the table in front of Latoya and E-Money, he took in her beauty as well.

"Will that be all Mama Toya?" The scullion asked in a sexy ass voice that drove E-Money mad.

"Yes baby, thank you," Latoya retorted.

"You're welcome," the scullion said. Before leaving, she leaned into Latoya and gave her a passionate, slow kiss. *Damn it is true, this bitch got pussy on deck,* E-Money thought.

"Are you okay?" Latoya asked with a smile on her face on ogling E-Money, feeling the intensity of E-Money's eager chemistry. Only if he knew what she had in store for him, he'd be across the table in a heartbeat.

━━

Inside Bobby's office at the chop shop/Bobby's Rims, Bobby gave the trio the real game to the cocaine distribution and the heroin. When he'd broke everything down to them and showed them the major loss that they've been in the blind on, D'Shawn wanted to bring Skip back to life just to kill him again. And the looks on Lee and Leon's face yielded the same prospect.

"Lee, D'Shawn, and Leon... there's a heavy load to carry. Skip made me 15% off of a kilo of cocaine, and 25% off of a kilo of heroin. Sell whatever to whomever you could trust with your dick, but make sure what's purchased from stock comes back to me. If you buy three kilos of heroin, then what am I expecting, D'Shawn?" Bobby asked randomly.

"25% in cut money," D'Shawn retorted.

"Why Leon?" Bobby asked.

"Because its 25% off of heroin," Leon retorted.

"And from two kilos of cocaine Lee, what am I looking for?"

"15%," Lee responded back to Bobby.

"Fair. Well then, we all have an understanding, I see. Skip had fifty men in clientele, ranging from Jersey to Florida. Two of you will get twenty-five apiece, and one of you will be a driver. Whichever one of you want to carry the responsibility of leavin' the country at times to sit down with my connect," Bobby said.

"I'll do that, since driving is my specialty," Lee took the job, smoothing things out for Bobby.

"Well I'll get with you two in a couple days," Bobby said pointing at D'Shawn and Leon on the leather sofa. "Meantime D'Shawn, handle business on Skip's phone, and transfer them quickly," Bobby said.

"Okay," D'Shawn and Leon said in unison.

━━

"Uhhh! Shit! Yes!" Latoya moaned out as E-Money entered her deep from behind doggy style. Her pussy smelled of strawberry, and tasted like peaches to E-Money. After eating the delicious lasagna, Latoya couldn't get enough of the handsome man at her table. She wanted him and he wanted her. When she made her bold move towards him at the table by kissing him, and directing his hands up her dress to feel her wetness, E-Money took control and ate her phat plump pussy on top of the table for dessert. When he brought her to her climax in under a minute, she knew she had a winner and had met her match.

Getting E-Money to the room was the most anxious that she'd ever been since high school. She was only twenty-eight years old and felt like she was fifteen again. E-Money took his time once in the bedroom; and opened her up from head to toe. Despite her being a lesbian, she still needed her back beat in from time to time, too. She couldn't believe how prodigious he was in the sack. And he was amazed at her pliability. She was definitely in shape. He was in a trance as he sent powerful strokes to her excessively wet mound.

Laying on his back as she rode his dick in the reverse cowgirl, Leon couldn't get enough of seeing his dick disappear inside of Nicole's phat pussy. If it wasn't for the distinctive tattoos on her body, at times he would swear that he was actually fucking Blac Chyna. *SMACK!* Slapping her on her succulent ass cheek and watching the aftermath amused him, too. He knew that he had a bad bitch, and also knew that he was seriously falling for her. Leon had no intention of letting her run back to her nigga. Whenever he did come home.

"You love this dick, huh?" Leon asked Nicole. Artistically while still keeping Leon's dick inside her pussy, she turned around to face him, simultaneously riding his dick. When she looked him in his eyes, he had his answer.

Despite the new lavish scenery, the bank account, and away from the slums and creatures, she was still unable to defeat the torment of depression. She'd just seen her doctor and the only thing good that he had to say was that her medication was doing a tremendous good job at a balancing out her T cells.

"I need my life back," she cried out.

Her boyfriend had just left again and wouldn't return until next week. She had made love to him, trying like every time to avoid him. She felt terrible how she was doing him. *He needs to know that he might be infected with HIV,* she thought sadly. *But how would I tell him... or should I make it seem as he gave it to me? But they have ways to find out the carrier,* she thought. She had no clue how to come forward and tell anybody of her illness, worst of all, her severe addiction to heroin. It assuaged her from her pain and she had no other way to make it disappear. Alone in her room with the door closed and locked, she enjoyed her privacy. She looked at the swollen vein from pumping her hand open and closed. She was naked alone with no pain soon. She injected herself with the syringe, and let the warm liquid flow through her veins.

"Ahhh! Yesss!" She exhaled, climaxing from how great it made her feel. *It's always the good shit that made me cum, and I have an ounce to go. Damn this shit.* "Uhhh! Uhh!" She purred out loud, rubbing her swollen clitoris, the stuck her fingers in her creamy pussy. "Yesss! Shit!" She moaned out while pleasing herself. She was too high to realize and notice that her menstruation had come on. This was the stage she loved being in, because she felt no pain.

CHAPTER 18

T-MAC HAD BEEN WAITING to hear back from his connect since yesterday. It was time for him to reup on his product and purchase the three kilos that he always came for.

"Baby, did you hear what happen in East Orange?" Tracy came into the bedroom nude inquiring of T-Mac. T-Mac was engrossed in his iPhone on YouTube checking out the new Kanye West hit.

"Nawl boo, what's goin' on?" T-Mac retorted never lifting his head up.

"Somebody ran in the gambling house on 151st and Spruce, and killed everything in there."

"Say what!" T-Mac exclaimed fully alert, after hearing gamble house. He knew the place well, because that's where he always picked up his product from his connect. Tracy had concern in her eyes as well, but absentmindedly, T-Mac had missed her worrisome ass, and had no clue that they were concerned about the same individual. When T-Mac pulled up the news date on his phone his mind went into a nimble, vagrant rollercoaster of what could of happen; when he saw the images from the chilling scene.

"FIVE FOUND DEAD INSIDE HOME!"

"Damn!" T-Mac exclaimed absentmindedly. He immediately

called his connect's phone to see what was up and to make sure that he wasn't one of the dead men being carried out the house in a black body bag. On the third ring, he picked up. T-Mac sighed hearing a connection.

"Yo, what's good?" A voice said that didn't belong to his connect, but sounded familiar.

"Skip...that's you?" T-Mac asked perplexed. When he looked over at Tracy, he saw that she was all in his business, something that he highly didn't tolerate. "Bitch, get out my business. Matter fact, I need some privacy!" T-Mac spat at Tracy.

"Fuck you nigga, and I got your bitch!" Tracy shouted throwing a pillow in T-Mac's face, then stormed from the room wrapped in a towel.

"I'll deal with you when I'm done," T-Mac said then resumed his conversation. "Hello," T-Mac spoke.

"Man, Skip ain't no longer in service."

"What do you mean nigga, where is Skip?" T-Mac asked perplexed.

"Man like I said, he no longer in service. How may I help you?" D'Shawn asked T-Mac.

"Nigga, do I know you, B?" Asked T-Mac trying to fit the voice of the person speaking with him with his gut feeling.

"You askin' too many questions, and not numbers homie."

"Man, I need my regular."

"Three of them will be ready. When you ready, come on 129th and Kentucky," said D'Shawn.

129th and Kentucky... that's D'Shawn's alley. Oh, shit.

"This D'Shawn, B?" T-Mac asked, finally placing the voice to its owner.

"It's not professional to scream out names, homie," D'Shawn spat.

"Man, I need three and a front home."

"No fronts, three or starve," D'Shawn retorted hanging up the phone.

"I can't believe this shit!" T-Mac screamed as he called Bean on speed dial.

"What's poppin', 5?" Bean answered.

"Man, meet me at the trap!" T-Mac yelled into the phone then hung up. He quickly got dressed and rushed out the door with his .44 Bulldog and red bandana.

If them niggas did anything to Skip, then that would be the call for war, T-Mac thought jumping in his BMW .745 and accelerating to the hood. When he was gone, Tracy tried calling and got an answer. *Thank God,* she thought then sighed.

"Hello," the caller said, that wasn't Skip.

"Where's Skip?" she asked perplexed.

"Skip's no longer with us, so don't call no more," said the caller then hung up on Tracy. *What the fuck is going on?* She thought perplexed and highly worried about Skip's safety.

When T-Mac pulled up to the 129th and Kentucky, him and Bean stepped out of the car, and walked up to the rowhouse. Chase stayed inside the car in the back seat, ready to send a deadly fusillade if shit popped off. Before T-Mac could knock, the door swung open and there, both enemies stared each other in the eyes.

"What's good, my nigga? You coming emptyhanded," said D'Shawn, seeing no money or duffel bag with their cash to purchase the three kilos that the regular gets.

"Man, what's good with Skip?" T-Mac exclaimed, as Lee appeared in the doorway with D'Shawn with an ominous look on his face.

"Nigga if that's what you here fo' then I suggest you to beat your feet. Now when you talking 'bout money nigga, we can deal," D'Shawn spat impertinently. "Now please leave my shit, B, because y'all niggas—" Before D'Shawn could finish, he had to weave a cheap shot from Bean. He moved with agility and connected a nimble two-piece to Bean's face, causing him to stumble backwards down the stairs.

It was on.

When T-Mac tried to catch D'Shawn from the blind side, Lee was there on time. He stole on T-Mac, dropping him instantly. Things weren't looking good for T-Mac and Bean. Niggas on the block came in a hurry to Lee and D'Shawn's aid. Chase tried to seize the opportunity to knock off a couple foes. When he stuck his body out the window aiming at the crowd with his mini .14, he was taken off-guard by T Gutta, who was running to assist from the next street over.

BOC! BOC! BOC!

"Arghhh shit!" Chase screamed as the bullet pierced through his shoulder, causing him to drop the mini .14. Chase was lucky unbeknownst T Gutta shot awkwardly due from running simultaneously shooting, or else Chase would have been a dead man; like T Gutta strongly intended. D'Shawn was sitting on Bean's chest pounding him, as Lee held a toe to toe combat with T-Mac, who was a great fighter. When the shots came, a lot ran for cover. Females had their phones out recording the riot and putting footage on Facebook. Miraculously, Bean had slid himself under a car, away from D'Shawn's pounding.

"Bitch ass nigga, you runnin' now!?" D'Shawn screamed in rage. Bloods from 33rd and Santa who'd caught wind to the brawl on 129th and Kentucky had come four SUVs deep, but were held up by the niggas holding down 129th and Kentucky, before they had time to jump out their SUV's. They were sandwiched and beaten with bottles, bricks, and any weapon the block had available. Seeing T-Mac's momentum fluctuate on Lee, D'Shawn stole T-Mac, knocking him out cold.

"JAKES!" Someone screamed, alerting everyone that the police had arrived in unmarked Dodge Ram trucks. Everyone scattered like rats, only a few being apprehended who couldn't get away. D'Shawn watched Bean and one of his Blood brothers carry an unconscious T-Mac to a SUV and peel off. D'Shawn knew that it wasn't over with, and that him and T-Mac would see each other again. They had no choice, because D'Shawn was now the new connect. The only one who wasn't there to participate was Leon, and D'Shawn and Lee just knew that would have been just too much Jenkins beating for T-Mac and Bean.

━━━

"Awww shit!" Chase screamed out in devastating pain as the street doctor tried removing the bullet from his shoulder. Fortunate for him, he was struck only one time. The doctor was an ex-surgeon who'd lost his license after being convicted of tax fraud. His name was Dean, and he was an old white man in his sixties.

"Stop bitching, we're almost done," said Dean to Chase, who laid on the kitchen table in the trap.

"Fuck you old man, aww!"

T-Mac sat in the living room with a frozen steak over his swollen eye. Bean was out looking for a man to purchase the three kilos, because they desperately needed product. More than twenty junkies had come to the trap, leaving sadly empty handed, and very disappointed. *We need this product or the clientele will go into them niggas turf,* T-Mac thought.

"I gotta kill this nigga," T-Mac mumbled to himself.

"Awww shit!" Chase screamed out in pain.

"There it goes!" Dean exclaimed pulling the bullet out of Chase with tweezers.

"Now all we have left to do is patch you up!" said Dean smiling at a semi-conscious Chase.

━━━

"Girl look at this shit!" Yalunder shouted to Varshay as she hurried, and sat down at the lunch table in the school's cafeteria. Yalunder showed her phone to Varshay, who was munching on a mouth full of fries. She saw a frozen footage on Facebook then tapped the screen to play the recording.

"Oh my God, it's going down, Bean just swung on D'Shawn; and the stupid nigga missed!" The girl with the camera screamed.

A stampede of niggas were shown coming from everywhere running towards the fight, where Varshay saw D'Shawn on top of Bean pounding on him. Then she observed T-Mac and D'Shawn's cousin Lee going at each other blow for blow.

"What the hell is going on, on 129th and Kentucky?" Yalunder inquired in total shock.

"What's up baby?" Tony P said sitting down at the table next to Yalunder. He too was in his phone attentively, like everyone else in the entire cafeteria.

BOC! BOC! BOC!

"Oh my God, where is D'Shawn!" Varshay screamed frantically, causing heads to turn in her direction. She could no longer see the altercation because the scary ass camera girl was running away at the sounds of the shots to avoid a stray bullet. Varshay quickly with trembling hands pulled out her iPhone and called D'Shawn's phone. When he picked up on the third ring, she exhaled a stressful sigh.

"Hello?"

"Baby, are you okay?" Varshay asked nervously.

"Most definitely I'm okay, just a little scratch baby... Nothing too major," D'Shawn retorted, nonchalantly, putting a smile on Varshay's face.

"Are Lee and Leon okay as well?"

"Baby, we Jenkins, we'll always be okay. Plus, Leon missed out on the fun," D'Shawn said.

"I love you," Varshay said letting it slip, but it was too late to put it back into the jar, and she meant it. Yalunder and Tony P both stared at her with shocked looks upon their face but were the least surprised.

Damn, that was deep, Yalunder thought.

D'Shawn was taken off-guard, but he knew that she meant every word of it. With a smile on his face, he spoke, killing the eerie silence.

"I love you too, and more than you love me."

Damn that's deep, Yalunder thought again. The smile that swept across Varshay's face was bright enough to blind the entire lunch room.

"Okay, Mrs. Jenkins!" Yalunder exclaimed.

"Shut up!" Varshay said blushing and on the verge of tears as she disconnected the call.

"Damn, I love that nigga fo'real. T-Mac done finally got what he had already waiting on him," Varshay exclaimed.

"Yeah... I just wish that I was there to pound his ass, too," Tony P retorted spitefully.

"Don't worry, my baby handled all our light weight," Varshay said then stuffed her mouth with fries.

CHAPTER 19

"So, you want me to go and put my face as y'alls product. After y'all done brought it to buddy," J Mack said to Bean. He was the head member of the Valentines Bloods in Newark; a distinctive Blood from T Mac who was a 9 Tech Blood member. Despite being under the same red bandana, there were still indifferences amongst them. T-Mac and J Mack just didn't mix. Neither of them could do away with their ego potency problem. As far as the west side of Newark was concerned, they cared less of what went down in the east of Newark.

"Man, it ain't like we not goin' to look out J Mack," Bean said ready to explode. He knew just as well as J Mack that shit was about to get ugly. Chase most definitely would retaliate and get back for being shot.

"Say... why did y'all bring problems to D'Shawn in the first place?" J Mack inquired.

Bean didn't want to explain to J Mack the real motive from T-Mac perspective. He would never betray his homie, and put T-Mac's business in the streets, despite how it already looked. T-Mac's vengeance revolved from D'Shawn's relationship with Varshay. So Bean gave the story of Skip's sudden disappearance. Something that he wished he would have never done.

"So, a nigga got killed, kidnapped or whatever. He tells y'all that shit still good and y'all go over to start a quarrel with the man, and get a brother shot and some snatched up by the jakes. Something don't make sense on that, twelve homie," J Mack said standing up from the sofa to cut off the television.

J Mack stood tall at six-feet-six-inches, 230lbs solid muscle, with a very swarthy complexion. He was a beast. He was an extremely humble, respected guy in his mid-thirties and dealt with trouble with prudence. When he cut the TV off and looked at Bean, Bean knew where things were going. J Mack was his affiliated brother and lying amongst them was cardinal.

"Give it to me raw homie, is this 'bout D'Shawn fucking with T-Mac's bitch?"

"Do it look like I'm backin' him on some hoe shit Blood!" Bean raised his voice, offensively.

"Raise your voice at me in my shit again Bean, and we are goin' to have our own problems, homie," J Mack said, sternly.

Bean knew that he stood no chance against J Mack. The nigga had hands the size of a baseball glove, and had a heavyweight boxing title.

"Man, it's simple, we give you the money to go get the shit for us."

"No, I'll do it and reestablish y'alls business. If it's not about feelings, then it shouldn't be any problems to squash the shit," J Mack stated.

"Man, Chase ain't gonna squash a nigga shootin' him," Bean said.

"Well keep us Valentines out of that shit, because it don't smell right. Chase don't know who the fuck shot him!" J Mack spat.

Damn we need this man, Bean thought. He knew that Chase would have no understanding. *We'll get back Chase,* Bean ultimately thought.

"I'll talk with Chase, Blood," Bean finally resolved.

"When you do, come with the and money and we'll all go over to D'Shawn," J Mack said.

"Oh my gosh, D'Shawn!" Varshay purred as D'Shawn rapidly thrust in and out of her pussy deeply. Her legs were locked behind his back, and her back arched, so that she could stimulate her clitoris and G spot simultaneously with each stroke. They were at D'Shawn's opulent suite in West Newark and it was their grand opening, making love in their king-sized bed for the first time.

Damn, this dick is good! Varshay thought as she began gyrating her hips simultaneously, matching his powerful strokes.

"Uhh! Uhh! Uhhh!" Varshay moaned out gasping for air as D'Shawn entered her deeply. *This man is fucking the shit out of me,* she thought as she came to her third climax. "Awww babeee!" Varshay exhaled vibrating as the electrifying orgasm took her to the planet of ecstasy.

"Arghhh!" D'Shawn moaned out as he shot his load inside Varshay. When she felt his load inside her, she grabbed him and kissed him passionately.

"I love you," she said, pecking his lips holding onto his sweaty body tightly.

"I love you too, baby," D'Shawn retorted sincerely.

After school, she'd come over to find D'Shawn asleep in just his Polo briefs. She quietly undressed and awoke him with the best head in her book. He was exhausted from running in the streets, and she knew exactly what he needed to be rejuvenated.

"Baby I love you, what have you done to me?" Varshay said as she climbed on top of D'Shawn after the longest round of their love making. Boyz II Men emanated in the background at a low volume from his surround system.

"I love you more... and it's what you done to me?" D'Shawn retorted.

Varshay smiled then kissed him softly on his lips again, tasting the sex of their combined bodily fluids.

"So tomorrow is graduation and my dad is miserable at the prospect of me possibly movin' in with you," said Varshay.

"Possibly huh?" D'Shawn exclaimed.

"Boy stop getting in yo' feelings, I know where my place at. If I didn't then I wouldn't have a key for myself," Varshay stated confidently.

D'Shawn knew that Varshay's father deeply despised him, because he was into the streets and not an attendant of Harvard University. At times, he would place himself inside Mr. Lewis' shoes.

"If I had a beautiful daughter like you, I'll have my cork up my ass too, with a string attached to your every movement," D'Shawn said sarcastically.

"Boy, you so stupid!" Varshay erupted in laughter.

She had the most adorable laugh ever to D'Shawn. And a laugh that he wanted to perpetually have around him. *Damn, what has this girl done to me?* D'Shawn thought.

Varshay saw the look in his eyes and knew that he was engrossed in mesmerism. With no need for words, she immersed below the covers, and placed his dick in her mouth, rebirthing another erection.

"Damn, ma," D'Shawn purred as he watched the covers go up and down like the beating to his heart that carried the love for her.

━━

Tracy's curiosity had got the best of her, worrying about Skip's sudden evading. She knew that he wasn't one of the victims killed in the gambling house on 151st and Spruce, because all their names were released. Tracy hopped in a cab and took it all the way into East Orange. Where she then caught a bus to Skip's side of town. When she got to Skip's section, she halted another cab straight to his residence.

"Thank you, sir," Tracy said to the Arab cab driver after paying him with the cash for the ride and tips.

"You're welcome ma'am," the Arab retorted.

She saw his Range Rover so she knew that he was home. *This nigga probably got a bitch in there,* Tracy thought as she strutted towards the front door in her heels and mini-dress that was skin tight. She prepared to put on her best hood rat defense. When she got closer, she could see clearly through the living room, and what she saw took the breath out of her.

"Oh my God!" she panicked instantly as she looked at the vandalism from her unobstructed view of the living room. The gorgeous trees that covered his front door and living room would prevent anyone from seeing the vandalism. Stuck in her tracks, and afraid to move, she began to regret ever making the trip. But instead of walking away, she absentmindedly pulled out her phone from her Louis Vuitton purse and called 911.

"911, what seems to be the emergency?" 911 dispatch inquired.

"Umm... I'm at 2782 Dr. And I want to report a suspicious, possible home invasion. My friend might be in trouble."

"Ma'am what's your friend's name?"

"Tyrone Stany," Tracy responded.

"Okay ma'am, help will be there shortly. Please, stay out of the way of any danger," 911 dispatch said. *Damn I hope he alright,* Tracy thought as she hung up on 911.

Tracy turned away and hastily walked away from Skip's residence. She had no clue why she was walking away, but something in her gut had told her to get as far away as she could from Skip's house. Tracy flagged down another cab, and repeated the same process that got her there. *I just hope he's alright, because I need to talk to him 'bout this baby. He's the only nigga who's been fucking me without any protection. So there's no denying this baby,* Tracy thought as she made her way back to Newark.

———

"Girl, you done found you some dick and can't even give a bitch no head or pussy," Nicole said to Latoya half-kidding. Despite of having Leon as her pounder, she still wanted Latoya's unique head game.

"Oh please bitch, you so stuck on Leon that you don't even spread them legs for me no more," Latoya retorted.

"Because E-Money always in your bed when I come in. I don't want to disturb you and your man."

"He's our man... The man who's going to handle business fo' the both of us," Latoya said.

"I still don't want to disturb y'all."

Then join us, Latoya thought. "Aww! I'm so sorry baby, c'mere," Latoya exclaimed as she reached out and grabbed Nicole in an embrace.

They were in the kitchen preparing a salad for dinner. Latoya held Nicole in a warming embrace sensing her sexual frustration. She began to kiss Nicole slowly and passionately. Feeling herself arousing, she started kissing and sucking on Nicole's neck, knowing her hot spots.

"Ummm, Latoya!" Nicole purred out in ecstasy as Latoya pulled down on her red maxi dress and caressed Nicole's erected nipples and breast.

"Ahhh!" Nicole exhaled as Latoya placed her brown nipple in her mouth and sucked passionately.

"Latoya baby, that feels good," Nicole moaned out.

She rubbed her hands through Latoya's curls and inhaled the sweet smell of her strawberry Olay's body wash and conditioner. *Damn, I love this bitch,* Nicole thought as Latoya kissed her and pulled her down to the immaculate green marble tile floors. On the floor, Latoya wasted no time immersing beneath Nicole's Macys dress to find her with no panties on, and the redolence of her sexual arousal intensifying, and enticing. When Latoya spread her pussy lips apart and swiped her tongue inside her pussy. Nicole arched her back, and grabbed on to the back of Latoya's head.

"Ohh shit!" Nicole moaned out.

"Eat this pussy baby!" She purred gyrating her hips. When

Latoya put her tongue on Nicole's clitoris and ran he tongue in figures of eights. An electrifying wave of ecstasy caused her to orgasm.

"Uhhh! Shit!" She shouted letting her load fall into Latoya's mouth.

"Baby I love you," Nicole moaned out to Latoya, panting.

"I love you too, baby," Latoya retorted.

Damn this bitch needs to let E-Money join us, Latoya thought as she continued to please Nicole. She badly wanted to turn up their romance. And had plans to maneuver her dream to reality.

"Oh shit, B look at this shit!" Chase screamed from the living room looking at the news coverage in East Orange, NJ, and the picture next to the house that the body bag was being removed from.

"B... that's Skip, turn it up!" Said Bean with a furious look on his face.

"Early today a suspicious call was placed indicating the amiss chilling scenery of the home behind me. When authorities arrived on the scene, they quickly discovered the vandalism of the home that was evident from an unobstructed view in the living room. The authorities moved with caution and rammed the door, where they stumbled on the gruesome two badly decomposing bodies of Tyrone Stany and Celeste Trumen. Tyrone, who goes by the street name Skip, is believed to be a drug kingpin who was supplying the East Coast with innumerable amounts of large heroin and cocaine drops. The authorities, despite their speculation, have yet gathered enough to indict Stany before his murder. At this moment, the authorities are ruling this homicide as a drug deal gone bad, and assuming that Celeste Trumen was at the wrong place at the wrong time. If anyone has information on any lead suspects, please call tips line 1 800 TIPS in Newark. I am Cindy Cole reporting live from Channel 8 News in East Orange, New Jersey," the beautiful black reporter stated.

"Damn yo, them niggas just muscled the game. What's stopping us from taking it from them?" Asked Chase.

"For them to muscle and still putting the same quality of product out. Then that means—"

"They either got his plug or stash," T-Mac said cutting Bean off.

"So what you thinking of, nigga?" Asked Bean seeing the contemplative look on T-Mac's face.

"We'll lay on them niggas, and see which it is," T-Mac said, gladsome that he'd made the prudent call.

Not everything is solved by war, sometimes you had to lay and watch, T-Mac thought retrospectively of his father giving him the game at fifteen years old, when he decided to gang bang and become a Blood.

<hr>

Sitting in his enormous, luxurious antique-fashioned living room at his 2.5-million-dollar mansion in West Orange, NJ, Bobby and his new crew had just finished watching a rerun of the news of Skip's discovery. There was no evidence to tie any of them to a crime, but the advice still had to be given. Bobby knew the streets too well to underestimate them or anyone. *A strong man could be weak tomorrow despite being strong today,* Bobby thought.

"Well there's no links, but you must play it safe. D'Shawn if, and I'm only hypothetically speakin', but if by chance the authorities come to you and ask you—"

"It'll never happen. I know my right to remain silent and so do Lee and Leon," D'Shawn said to Bobby confidently cosigning for his two cousins' tenacity of their rights as well.

"Good, that's why I like you three. I have plans to bring you guys farther in this game than what you are seeing now," Bobby said, meaning every word he'd just told them.

"Lee...come sunrise, you'll be booking a private jet for your first meetin' with my connect. I hope that you're ready to enjoy beautiful Saudi Arabia," Bobby exclaimed, lighting up, an elated, ecstatic smile on his face.

"Hell fuck yeah I'm ready!" Lee exclaimed ecstatically. Lee had no clue what it was like to leave the country. Bobby searched the faces of D'Shawn and Leon, looking for and old common foe, that could never manipulate him. But when he saw that his nemesis was nowhere in the room, he became more content with the crew he had. Because envy had no home amongst the trio. The looks on D'Shawn and Leon's faces were the looks of mutual happiness. *Soon I'll have them beyond riches,* Bobby thought.

It was midnight when Bean had pulled up to the apartment complex in a Dodge Durango the color of Ebony. He was on a forbidden side of town, the Crips turf. So, he was extremely furtive as he spent some quality time with a beautiful bitch named Samantha. She was five-foot-four, 120lbs, the epitome of a Coke bottle frame, who looked like Lil' Kim in the face.

"Well daddy, I guess I'll see you tomorrow, I really enjoyed myself tonight. I wish I could stay the night, but I have to be at work in the morning." Samantha said.

They'd been together all evening laid up in a hotel fucking each other's brains out, until exhaustion.

"That's okay ma, I'll be back tomorrow to drop you some more cash off okay."

"Thank you, daddy," Samantha exclaimed then reached over and kissed Bean on the lips, simultaneously rubbing on his dick through his jeans. Samantha immersed below and unfastened Bean's belt. She then removed his Glock .40 and rested it on the driver's floor. When she pulled out Bean's erected dick and placed it in her mouth, she deep throated him until she gagged two times. Bean closed his eyes at the sweet fellation.

When Bean opened his eyes, he saw a gang of Crips, about six of them, running towards the SUV.

"Oh shit!" Bean screamed as he shoved Samantha away vigorously and reached for his Glock .40 on the driver's floor. He never had the chance to come back up, and he was grateful, because the shots that came through the windshield were coming straight for his head. Samantha began screaming hysterically, that quickly became irksome to Bean, as she stayed low below the dashboard.

BOC! BOC! BOC!

They ambushing me! Bean thought as the bullets riddled the SUV, taking out his windows.

"Fuck!" he shouted, starting up the SUV, throwing it in gear, and smashing on the gas. He stayed immersed below the dashboard as he swerved, trying to flee from the ambush.

SMASH!

Bean crashed into a parked car with the shots now behind him. Samantha continued to scream as he reversed the SUV. Unable to take anymore, Bean turned the gun on Samantha and shot her twice in the head. Fortunately, he'd found room to escape from the fusillade in the wrecked Durango.

"Dammit... close call!" Bean shouted, then began laughing hysterically. When he made it to a safer location he dumped the Durango that belonged to a junkie that allowed him to rent it for a day, and halted the first cab in sight.

"Where to, partner?" the black man inquired of Bean.

"East Newark on 33rd and Santa," Bean retorted, then laid back in the seat, grateful to still be alive. He hated killing Samantha, but in the perilous situation she'd quickly become a distraction that could have easily got him killed. Samantha was a good girl who'd just got caught up with the wrong nigga. *I had to get one of them mother-fuckas... and she was one of them, in my eyes,* thought Bean. Now he had to find the junkie, because he as well had to die, before the authorities found Samantha, and linked the truck back to the owner.

CHAPTER 20

"AND OUR NEXT graduate of West Orange high is Tiffany Dawson!" The Principal of West Orange High proclaimed, as the crowd in the auditorium gave a tremendous applause.

When Tiffany, a gorgeous swarthy complexioned girl sashayed to the podium in her red graduation gown, the ovation intensified.

"Thank you so much!" She cried into the mic, smiling, and waving to the crowd, then went to stand on stage along with the other graduates.

"And our next graduate of West Orange High is Yalunder Jordan!" The Principal proclaimed.

When Yalunder sashayed into the applauding auditorium, she was in tears. She'd finally done what her mother expected of her. And seeing her mom and little brother Travis clapping their hands along with the crowd was the best feeling in the world. Someone in the crowd caught her eyes that turned her mood sour briefly, because she definitely wasn't about to let no busta ruin her day. She could've won an Oscar for how she hid her distaste for the individual. *What the fuck is he here for?* Yalunder wanted to know as she stared at T-Mac in the crowd. When she looked for D'Shawn, she caught him mean mugging T-Mac from across the room. *Please Lord, don't let him start no shit,* Yalunder thought as she received her diploma then went to stand with the rest of the graduates.

"And our next graduate of West Orange High is our very own prom queen, Varshay Lewis!" proclaimed the Principal. When Varshay sashayed on stage, the crowed intensified in ovation. There was whistling and shouts of applause for Varshay as she went to the podium to accept her diploma. She too had seen T-Mac in the crowd, standing and clapping with everyone else. But she kept her eyes on her man, as she undulated across the stage.

What the fuck is he doing here!? Varshay wanted to know as she went to stand next to Yalunder.

"Why is he here?" Varshay mumbled to Yalunder in hushed tones.

"Your guess is as good as mine," Yalunder retorted back in hushed tones.

The Principal, Mrs. Morgan, was a beautiful black woman in her late forties, but looked every bit of thirty. She called out eighteen more students before calling her surprise to the stage.

"People, our next student to graduate and desert to tonight's celebration—"

Desert means last, where is Tony P? Yalunder thought, curious like others.

"People, this student who was the best athlete to ever come through West Orange High my entire fifteen years here as a Principal —" Yalunder smiled, already knowing like everyone else, whom the Principal was talking about.

That's right... the best, Yalunder thought.

"Our first state title came from the amazing performance of this talented individual—"

"Tony P! Tony P! Tony P!" Folks in the crowd shouted.

"People not everyone gets a chance, and I'm proud to know that our quarterback has accepted a full scholarship to the University of Miami! I would like to call Tony Pierre to the stage as our last graduate at West Orange High!" The Principal shouted into the mic over the overwhelming applauding.

Fuck nigga! T-Mac thought spitefully. It was because of him that his bitch was all in the next man's grill.

"Oh my gosh!" Yalunder exclaimed, surprised of the news, and happy for her man. Tears instantly cascaded down her face, as Tony P walked on stage, blowing Yalunder a kiss, causing her to blush highly.

"Thank you so much, and I mean thank the entire staff here at West Orange High, who pushed me encouragingly, to my best ability, and gave my potential a chance," Tony P said into the mic, pausing for a second for the ovation to settle down. "Most of all, I would like to thank Coach Harris for all the help and prudent advice, for it has made me a man in all aspects," Tony P continued.

"Girl, looks like your man going to Miami!" Varshay screamed to Yalunder in the midst of the exhilarating ovation as Yalunder dried her tears away with her hand.

"You so damn emotional!" Varshay exclaimed.

"So bitch, you would too. I can't help it, and don't act like D'Shawn don't make you cry," Yalunder said.

―

Outside in the parking lot Varshay held onto D'Shawn's arm intertwine, while walking towards D'Shawn's brand new silver Range Rover sitting on 28" Lexani Leo's rims.

"So, are we going to the celebration for Tony P, or do you have a particular celebration in mind?" Varshay asked.

"Nawl, but we could—"

"Yo D'Shawn let me have a word with you, homie... man to man," T-Mac spoke from behind D'Shawn and Varshay.

"Really T-Mac?"

"I ain't talking to you, I'm talking to ya man," T-Mac spat standing with three of his Blood brothers, none of them who

D'Shawn had recognized. He knew that T-Mac hung with Bean and Chase heavy, and to see that neither of them was present was something unordinary to D'Shawn and Varshay. D'Shawn was definitely strapped and wouldn't hesitate taking much as he could, if all if he had to.

"What you have to say could be said in front of her," D'Shawn said with an ominously look upon his face.

"She may be my ex—"

"I ain't shit to you nigga, so please dismiss me," Varshay spat angrily. T-Mac looked at her then slightly chuckled briefly, before D'Shawn was up in his grill.

"Give me a reason nigga," D'Shawn said face-to-face with T-Mac who stood solidly. His Blood brothers had revealed themselves too early, exposing that they were stopped when they flinched at D'Shawn's nimble stand down with T-Mac.

"Homie, let's not get to carried away... we are not here fo' no problems."

"Well let's keep it like that and now get on with what you want with me," D'Shawn spat, looking T-Mac in his undaunted eyes.

"Man, I need them three—"

"Man, I already talked with J Mack and told him what it was. I'mma fuck with y'all niggas as long y'all keep it business," D'Shawn said.

"That's no pressure B," T-Mac retorted.

"How soon?"

"Now," T-Mac retorted.

"In three hours, I'll hit you to make that happen," D'Shawn said then turned on his heels with Varshay back on his arm. *This nigga is a boss out here,* Varshay concluded. It didn't take a rocket scientist to understand the cryptic dialogue. *T-Mac was asking D'Shawn for a chance and he gave it to him,* Varshay thought.

"But let him tell it T-Mac is the man," Varshay said with emphasis and a smirk on her face.

"He is the man... the man that will bring me the money I needed," D'Shawn retorted, navigating the Range Rover out the school zone.

"I'm proud of you, baby," D'Shawn said to Varshay.

"I can't believe that I made it, D'Shawn," Varshay said wiping the cascading tears from her face. Her parents had left after she'd received her diploma, leaving D'Shawn alone. They were happy for their daughter, despite her father still being adamant about D'Shawn.

"So what did your father say?" D'Shawn asked as if he could feel her thoughts.

"He still tells me to give us more time together before we move in together."

"What did you tell him?" D'Shawn retorted.

Varshay preferred to show him rather than tell him. She immersed her seat and slid over to D'Shawn. She lifted up his black t-shirt then removed his .44 Bulldog and placed it on the passenger's floor. Varshay licked inside his navel simultaneously unfastening the belt to his True Religion jeans. She pulled his erected dick through his Polo briefs slot, then slowly gave him head. The fellation that she was administering had him swerving slightly out of traffic.

"Damn baby!" D'Shawn moaned out as Varshay sucked his dick like her favorite lollipop. In five minutes tops, Varshay had him climaxing, shooting his load into her mouth, where she thoroughly swallowed every drop.

"I told him that D'Shawn is my man and I belong with him, and in his arms every night," Varshay spoke truthfully.

"You didn't tell him that!" D'Shawn said turning the low volume of the Usher down in the car system.

"Bet me a hundred dollars," Varshay retorted.

"I believe you, baby," said D'Shawn then blasted the Usher hit Nice 'n' Slow.

"What the fuck you mean you can't do this no more!" Yalunder yelled at Tony P from across the other side of the bed.

After making love to her, he'd came out and told her flat that he wanted out of the relationship. Yalunder wasn't taking it how he'd expected her to. She erupted in rage, throwing anything that she could put her hand on at him. It fucked Tony P up mentally, but he managed to stay strong and not give in. She didn't care that she was a guest under his roof. Tony P was her man and she wasn't about to just let him walk away from their relationship that they'd been so content in.

"How could you do us like this, Tony P... why?!" Yalunder cried out, falling to the ground exhausted from the painful bombshell. Her world had turned upside down in one happy night that suddenly turned cold. *And the least he could do is tell me he can't carry on a long-distance relationship,* Yalunder thought. "Tony P baby, I will move to Miami, whatever it takes. Just please don't walk away from me. I love you too much!" Yalunder cried out with a snotty running nose, completely bent out of shape.

I can't believe that he is trying to leave me, she thought.

"Baby I told you, it's not you, Yalunder. I just don't want to deal with hurtin' you—"

"What, I was just a high school fling to you, Tony P? Is that what you are telling me huh!?" She cried out.

"No, you're not a fling. College is different, and more opportunities will be in my face. I can't commit to being faithful like that, baby," Tony P explained truthfully.

"I told you that I would move to Miami!" she said between clenched teeth.

"And I told you that I don't want to be with you anymore. Since you can't fathom, I'll give you time to soak it in," Tony P said walking out of the room, tired of going back and forth with a no-win situation. He was adamant on his decision and there weren't enough tears in the world to change his mind. He was going to Miami a free man to play ball, then off to the pros. Being committed during this transitional moment in life was just not fitting in his plans.

When she heard the door close, she broke down hysterically. She just knew that Tony P was gone. Tony P was the only man that she'd ever let have her heart. He showed her what her worth was as a woman. When she needed someone to call on other than Varshay, it was him. When she dreamt of getting married with kids, it was him standing at the altar. *I know now why the nigga stayed pulling out... he'd been planning to leave me all along*, Yalunder thought. *He didn't want no kids with me, he played me.*

Getting on the bed and balling into a fetal position, Yalunder closed her eyes to find sleep, hoping that it was a dream, and when she awoke that Tony P would be in her arms, and the pain gone.

Detective David Morris was a black man in his mid-forties, and East Orange NJ's best homicide detective. He'd finally got the requested phone records of the 911 call made reporting the suspicion of Tyrone Stany and Celeste Trumen's murders.

"Her name is Tracy Miller and she's originally from Opa Locka, Miami, Florida," Detective Michele Cummings exclaimed to her partner. Michele Cummings was a black woman in her thirties, and very attractive, from Harlem. She started in Narcotics, until her undercover role played out, almost costing her life at the hands of a vicious drug lord who'd discovered her true identity.

"Do we have a ping location?" Asked Detective Morris.

"As of now, her phone is off," Detective Cummings exclaimed. "But I will keep on it," Detective Cummings said.

As she left he couldn't help staring at her scintillating petiteness. She was the color of maple brown sugar and stood curvaceous at five-feet-five-inches, 130lbs. She was the best partner he'd ever had of his twenty years in the field. Detective Morris looked at the phone records of Tracy Miller and began his inquiry dialogue in his head of what questions he would definitely ask as he sat in his comfortable chair and rubbed his eyes from a long, drudging sixteen-hour shift. *I think I'mma call it a night and resume in the morning*, Detective Morris thought yawning.

▭

D'Shawn and Leon both pulled up to the Cassidy Park on 20th and Amherst. It was midnight and the other party hadn't arrived yet. They both had on armored vests and carried mac-10s, fully loaded. When they saw the headlights sweep into the parking lot and accelerate towards them head on with their lights beaming, D'Shawn flicked on his high beams as well.

"B, these niggas clowning already. I say let's wash them and go," Leon said, ready to lay a nigga down.

The Suburban killed their lights first, then D'Shawn returned the favor.

"Stay here, when you see me walking back to the truck, engage the safe box," D'Shawn said to Leon then exited the Range Rover.

When D'Shawn walked up to the black Suburban, the window came down instantly.

"Get in on the passenger side" J Mack said. D'Shawn walked around to the passenger's and hopped inside. Expecting to see T-Mac and Bean in the back seat, it was only J Mack in the Suburban.

"Where is T-Mac and Bean?" D'Shawn asked perplexed.

"Them niggas had to handle something, they said they'll be present on the next go 'round," J Mack exclaimed.

On 129th and Kentucky the two gunmen emerged from the stolen midnight blue Explorer and knocked on the 2800 door to the rowhouse. When a guy named Juicy opened the door expecting a junkie ready to spend some money, he saw two masked gunmen staring at him with two gun pieces aimed at him.

"Back inside nigga, and don't even try that Hercules shit," one of the gunmen said to the right of him, while putting up one gun in his

waist band. Juicy was only twenty-one years old and knew the fundamentals to the game well. *Never back a jack move if you can't see
your own back,* Juicy thought retrospectively of an ol'school cat
named Jon Jon saying. Inside was his girlfriend Olivia in a back room,
and had no clue of the intruders. Juicy backed inside the house with
his hands up, showing that he was willing to cooperate.

"Where is the stash?" one of the intruders asked the one holding
two guns at him.

"In the kitchen, man," Juicy retorted, tremulously.

"Check the kitchen," one intruder said to the other, the one with
the two guns instantly made a dash for the kitchen.

"Who in here with you?"

"My girl, she in the back room," said Juicy.

"Let's go," the intruder said, grabbing Juicy by his dreadlocks and
pressing the Glock .19 to his head.

The intruder escorted Juicy to a back room where the girlfriend
was meant to be. When the intruder stepped into the room, he and
Juicy were surprised to find the room illuminating from a TV and
empty.

"Where the fuck she at nigga, you playing games!"

"Man, I don't—" Before Juicy could finish, his girlfriend Olivia
came from behind and jumped on the intruder's back.

"What the fuck!" the intruder screamed in rage. Juicy nimbly
turned around and struck the intruder in the face, catching him
between the nose. But the intruder still managed to let off two shots.

BOOM! BOOM!

The two shots hit Juicy in his chest dropping him to his death.

"Nooo!" Olivia screamed then gave the intruder a piece of
her mind.

"Awww! Bitch!" the intruder screamed in pain as Olivia clamped
her teeth down on the back of his neck, biting him deeply, and
drawing blood. He had no choice with her teeth deeply in his flesh.
He aimed the gun backwards and pulled the trigger.

BOOM! BOOM! BOOM!

Olivia immediately fell from his back as the slugs penetrated her scalp, killing her instantly. The intruder ran from the room holding his neck from the gushing wound caused by Olivia. She did quite a number on him.

"Man, what the fuck!" The intruder who'd rummaged the kitchen exclaimed halfway down the hall on his way to help his partner.

"Man, that hoe bit me, B!" The intruder exclaimed still holding on to his neck wincing in pain.

"Man let's go, I got everything!"

Together they exited the trap house and hopped in with their getaway driver. They were now ten kilos strong, which made D'Shawn and his crew ten kilos in debt and loss of $50,000 that was found in a black duffel bag.

―――

"Yo before you go, I want to talk with you 'bout some business," J Mack said as D'Shawn had the money and took J Mack's word that all $225,000 was in the duffel bag.

"What's good, B?" D'Shawn asked as he heard a distant siren.

"I'm thinking 'bout getting back in the boxing industry."

"Yo B, that's good!" D'Shawn exclaimed, effusively. Deep down, D'Shawn's passion for boxing was still in him, but to pursue it feeble, due to the entrapment in the street life. The fast life came more abundantly to him.

"Yeah, but I'm not getting back in the ring," J Mack said.

"What do you mean?" D'Shawn inquired, curiously.

"Man, I know the right people to get behind me and I know the right potential to support. Man, you have a nice ass set of hands and the agility that the sport needs. D'Shawn, you could come up out the streets before you get trapped," J Mack said.

"This what I do, man... I'm fond of boxing, it's been a dream to me. But at the end of the day, I'm just an overlooked statistic."

"So tell me what do the streets owe, that you can't build yourself up and prove the statistics wrong. The streets like checkers homie, take and give. Like you never know how the streets will unfold for you at the end of the day. You'll never know how the boxing industry would unfold for you until you try it," J Mack spoke encouragingly.

What he was saying was true and left D'Shawn in some contemplative thoughts. Sometimes he saw himself as a heavyweight boxer, but as quickly as it came, despondency would diminish his dream.

"Man, I will give you time to think 'bout what you want to do. Just know that you have a chance to turn this dirty money into the cleanest life that you could ever dream of. You could scream that the streets is all you know, and I'll bet you that you never dreamed of being the man you are now... How I see it is, if you could venture the game, then you could venture your dream by giving it a chance," said J Mack. "I'll be on speed dial." J Mack said putting the Suburban in drive indicating that the meeting was over.

It was transparent to D'Shawn that J Mack was trying to help him act on his dream, and back him. But D'Shawn was too deep in the street life to let go. Too complacent to see what was good for him as well.

"I'll hit you up in a couple days—"

CHAPTER 21

"GIRL, I don't believe he'll do something like that, did y'all fight?" Varshay asked Yalunder while lying in bed waiting on D'Shawn to come back home.

"I don't know why he doing it Varshay, I've been good to him..." Yalunder paused sniffing from constantly crying and trying to bridle her emotions.

"I love him and all he sayin' is that college is going to be a different scenery—"

"So y'all was some type of high school fling!" Varshay exploded, feeling offended and hurt with her friend.

"Varshay, I love him so much!" Yalunder cried out hysterically, breaking down.

Shit! Varshay thought.

It pained Varshay how her friend was hurt. She had no right to be going through what she was experiencing. *She is in pain, mentally riddled, and she needs me there by her. D'Shawn would understand if he came home and I was gone. I needed to make sure that my friend is okay,* Varshay thought, not wanting to be out and about when her man came back from handling business. *A woman has no business in the streets past midnight unless they're trickin' on the prowl, or looking for a man at some club, and ultimately out havin' a girl's night,* Varshay thought.

"Where are you Yalunder?" Varshay asked.

"I'm at his place" Yalunder retorted still crying.

"I'm coming to get you, so be ready. If he don't want you there, then you don't need to be there until y'all settle out what need to be settled," Varshay told Yalunder.

"Okay I'll pack all of my stuff, and be waiting for you," said Yalunder.

"On the way there I'mma stop at White Castle and grab some burgers."

"No onions for me bitch, and I need three of them," Yalunder exclaimed, grabbing ahold of her stuff.

"Okay girl, see you soon," Varshay retorted then hung up the phone.

"That's the Yalunder I know. We sure ain't 'bout cryin' over a nigga who got his mind made up already," Varshay said as she got out of bed and slipped into a mini Prada dress and a pair of Jordan's No. 23.

When D'Shawn and Leon turned on 129th and Kentucky, they were stunned to see all the red and blue lights flashing on police cruisers and unmarks.

"What the fuck!" D'Shawn exploded hammering the steering wheel.

"B, look like the jakes done hit the trap," Leon concluded transparently from seeing the innumerable police near their trap house.

Ain't this a bitch? Leon thought.

Instead of proceeding to approach the trap, D'Shawn pulled into the Arab corner store to survey the activity at a distance. The street was crowded with nosey neighbors and junkies. It wasn't until

D'Shawn took a closer look, that he'd realized that what they were staring at was not a raid. *Oh shit!* D'Shawn thought.

"B... that's crime scene tape roping off the trap!" D'Shawn exclaimed in bewilderment.

"Hell yeah B, that's crime scene tape, that means there's a—"

"A body near," they said in unison. When D'Shawn saw T Gutta, he rolled the window down to the Range Rover, and called him over.

"Yo T Gutta, check it out, B!"

T Gutta strutted over quickly to D'Shawn and from the look on his face, D'Shawn could tell that T Gutta was glad to see him.

"Yo son, you clean?" asked T Gutta.

"Yeah. What's going on? Why they in my trap?" D'Shawn asked.

"B, someone washed Juicy and his bitch, and left the door wide open—"

"Get the fuck out of here, B!" D'Shawn exclaimed frantically, once again hitting the steering wheel.

"B, is Juicy and Olivia washed up?" Leon asked, not wanting to believe his ears.

"Washed B... no hope," T Gutta retorted.

"Old man Buff say he caught the ass end of it. Say that it was a robbery."

Acourse it was a robbery, it's a damn trap house, D'Shawn thought.

"Where's Buff?" D'Shawn asked

"Buff's gone. I personally did him myself from ear-to-ear," T Gutta said gesturing with his hand striking his thumb across his throat indicating that he'd cut Buff's throat.

"Why?" D'Shawn asked.

"Because when I asked him who it was, he stuttered, shit his pants, then remain adamant so I sent him to his maker," T Gutta explained.

"Who'll be this stupid to hit us up like this?" Leon spat.

"Anybody who needed to come up, and knew where to come at," T Gutta retorted.

"You see any drugs or money come out?" D'Shawn asked T Gutta.

"B, you know robbers don't leave that stuff behind," T Gutta responded.

He was right, they come for one thing, and Juicy was there because Lee couldn't be. *Meaning if Lee would've been in the country... my cousin would be washed too,* D'Shawn thought.

"Leon, I got to check the shit out, my name is on the lease. Get out of here, I will call you when I'm done securing up the trap."

"Do you think that nigga T-Mac did this shit?" Leon asked.

"I can't say, but the nigga would be a good guess," D'Shawn retorted.

When he looked at his phone he saw that it was dead, which made it impossible to call Varshay. And made it only worse when he couldn't recall her number by memory.

"B, go tell Varshay what's going on and I'll call when I get a chance to," D'Shawn told Leon as he hopped out of the Range Rover.

"T Gutta, keep ya ears open, because you my new sergeant for 129th and Kentucky. This will never happen again," D'Shawn exclaimed then walked down to the crime scene.

◁▭▷

"Awww shit!" T-Mac screamed out as Tracy poured peroxide over the gruesome looking bite wound on his neck.

"Baby, you might have to see a doctor for real. You know what that nigga have," Tracy said to T-Mac as he sat on the bathroom toilet with the seat down, getting cared for by her.

Tracy was under the impression that T-Mac was in another brawl with some Crips and one of the niggas bit him trying to get T-Mac off his brother. When she inquired where it happened, he'd told her that it occurred in the parking lot of White Castle when trying to order some burgers.

Tracy had no reason to doubt his story. She knew T-Mac being a

Blood member caught on the wrong side of Brick City could result in death. So, he was a lucky man to be alive. He had no clue of her and Skip's relationship, she decided to put the baby on T-Mac.

He won't know how far along I am, shit he can't deny that he was fucking me, either. I just got to let him fuck me unprotected a couple times. Lord knows I can't raise a child by myself, Tracy thought as she applied some antibiotic cream to T-Mac's wound.

"Try to at least go tomorrow and get a detector shot," Tracy recommended, while rubbing T-Mac's shoulders.

"I will baby, okay," T-Mac said with his eyes closed loving the comforting feeling of Tracy's hands on his shoulders that seemed to assuage some of the pain.

When he opened his eyes, he saw the lustful look in her eyes and knew that she wanted some dick. Looking at her in the transparent lingerie that was being swallowed by her curves, he couldn't resist an erection. He had nothing on but his boxers after just jumping out the shower. He rubbed her stallion thighs all the way to her shaven phat pussy. Slowly, he removed her lingerie, see through panties, and turned her around backwards.

SMACK! The sound of T-Mac slapping her succulent ass echoed throughout the bathroom. T-Mac bent Tracy over at the waist, and stuck his tongue in her asshole.

"Uhh shit baby, that feels so damn good," Tracy purred as T-Mac ate her ass and fingered her pussy.

Tracy knew that T-Mac would make a good father. And that it may 'cause him to slow down his life before he ended up getting killed. Like all of her previous boyfriends, just when she thought that she had Skip, he was dead. And the same with Rolex. Some nigga killed Rolex because he was getting money on every corner. *T-Mac is a good man, though. I know he still loves that hoe Varshay. I don't see them getting back together, but I got to give it to the girl... that nigga D'Shawn is fine,* Tracy thought as she came to her climax.

"Ooh babe!" Tracy moaned out as her creamy load filled T-Mac's mouth, and smeared on his lips and goatee.

She quickly turned around and pulled T-Mac's briefs to his ankles. With her hands on his shoulders, she straddled him, slowly descending on his dick, filling her womb with all of his length. For the first time T-Mac had felt her insides without using a condom.

"Damn baby, you feel too good," T-Mac said in ecstasy.

"Do I really feel good, daddy?" Tracy asked tightening her pussy muscles.

"Yes you do, ma," T-Mac exclaimed as she gyrated her hips and rode his dick until he exploded inside her.

Got 'em! Tracy thought as T-Mac released inside her tunnel with his eyes closed. She was now in the class of all women who lied, telling a nigga that the baby was his when they knew themselves who the baby's father was. *We having a baby, T-Mac!* Tracy thought gladsomely that the expedient task was accomplished

━━━

"So you mean to tell me that Leon has the connect with the heroin and he's getting it from motherfuckin' Bobby who is straight out tellin' us that he is no longer in the game!" Latoya screamed out in a raging fit.

"Baby I could go and whack his ass—"

"What good will it do to whack him if we don't know where he getting it from, E-Money. If I had any clue of where he is getting it from, then he would've been dead the moment he cut me off," Latoya exclaimed then turned her attention back on Nicole.

"Bitch, tell me you knew this all the while!" Latoya shouted at Nicole, who gave Latoya an ominous look.

"You must be out your mind to charge me with that phony ass shit. If I had known, we wouldn't even be having this conversation, Latoya," Nicole said bitterly and rolling her eyes at Latoya not appreciating her questioning her loyalty.

"Bitch, don't get fucked up, you hear me huh!?" Latoya spat, as she grabbed Nicole around her neck with both hands, backing Nicole up against the wall with a death grip.

"Do you hear me, bitch. Don't you get slick with me, I am the motherfuckin'—"

"Latoya stop!" E-Money screamed trying to pry Latoya's death grip from around Nicole's neck. Nicole's face had turned purple and from the looks of it, she was semi-conscious.

"Bitch, I run this shit!" Latoya screamed, completely spazzed out.

"Latoya, stop before you kill her!" E-Money shouted, but Latoya couldn't hear him. She could only hear herself spasmodically engrossed on choking the skit out of Nicole. To break her out of the trance, E-Money quickly delivered two blows to Latoya's side, knocking the wind out of her, causing her to let go of Nicole's neck.

"Awww!" Latoya cried out, grabbing her side, and gasping for air. E-Money had caught Nicole before she had hit the ground. She was going head first.

"Why the fuck did you hit me in my ribs, E-Money!"

"Shut the fuck up before I hit you again. When I tell you to stop, I mean it. This is your friend, don't let your anger take control of you."

"Fuck that hoe," Nicole spat breathlessly, letting fresh air into her lungs.

"What you said, bitch!" Latoya said charging Nicole. But unlike last time, Nicole was prepared as she nimbly side-stepped Latoya, simultaneously delivering a two-piece to Latoya's face. She knew better than to let Latoya grab her. It wasn't a cat fight but it was amusing to E-Money, who decided to let them rough it out. The last thing he would do is let them kill each other. What E-Money didn't know was that the quarrelsome friends and lovers once every blue moon had their differences and cat fights. When both woman had each other by the hair and pounding one another on the head, E-Money laughed as they beat each other to exhaustion.

▭

"I just don't understand them niggas. A woman who don't see no man but them is the one they leave for a tramp," Yalunder exclaimed, while eating her burger on the passenger side of Varshay's new Range Rover that D'Shawn got her for graduation. Her phone unbeknownst recording their entire conversation.

"Trying to understand a man is like trying to understand life," Varshay said as she yielded to a red light.

"From my understanding, we are born to die," Yalunder gave her prospect on understanding life, compared to understanding men.

"My point exactly, who would ever understand that?" Varshay retorted, making her sententious point clear.

"So what am I supposed to do, Varshay?" Yalunder asked with tears cascading down her face. Varshay hated seeing her friend emotionally torn apart. When T-Mac did her wrong, Yalunder was the one encouraging her to move on. Now it was her time to help Yalunder.

"Do you remember how I got over T-Mac, Yalunder?"

Let the ball fall in my court! Yalunder thought.

"Are you really over him, I mean like do you still think of him?... He's your first," Yalunder inquired in Varshay with a question that caught her off-guard. They were friends and could talk about anything.

Do I still think of T-Mac? Varshay searched her heart. The same heart that T-Mac had broken and D'Shawn healed.

"Occasionally I do, but it's the way he did me, not like missing him," said Varshay. "Yalunder, I don't know, but I do know that what me and D'Shawn have makes me happy and—"

"Takes away the pain," Yalunder suggested.

"It does but—"

"Do you love D'Shawn?" Yalunder asked.

"Yes I do love him," Varshay retorted.

"I think that I could get over Tony P, but I'll still love him the same way you love T-Mac until this day!" Yalunder exclaimed.

"I guess I do still love him, because I can't stand to see him get hurt," Varshay retorted.

"He bust that cherry girl, you'll always love him!" Yalunder said. Both of them join in laughter, assuaging each other's pain. *I got this bitch. He was meant for me... the way he looks at me, I can't help it,* Yalunder thought, impishly.

CHAPTER 22

THE SUN WAS ardent in the east when the luxurious G5 jet landed at Saudi Arabia airport in the city of Riyadh. Lee looked on in awe at the breathtakingly intriguing sight of the ancient city. The men had beards like Osama Bin Laden and the women were covered in Muslim gowns, concealing their beauty behind face garments. When Lee emerged from the jet's flight of descending stairs caught up in adoration of the city and being absentminded, a dozen of Muslim men out of nowhere swarmed him with AK47s aimed at him.

"Hey man!" Lee shouted with his hands extended in the air to show that he was less of a threat.

These motherfuckas look like "ISIL," Lee thought.

The men had garment wrapped around their head and faces and wore black Muslim gowns. One of the men came closer to Lee and poked his rifle into Lee's side, then shouted something indiscernible to Lee in Arabic.

"Man, I don't know what you—"

Before Lee could finish, a black cotton bag was vigorously placed over his head and tied by a string.

"What the fuck!" Lee yelled agitated as his feet began to move unwillingly in a haste. As Lee was being placed in the back seat of a limousine, all he could think about was killing Bobby if he ever made it back to America. Men with AK47s wearing hijabs on their face was definitely not something that Lee expected.

The entire ride to their destination was quiet. And all Lee could do was listen, and think of ways to escape. *Just like on TV, these moth-afuckas take hostages like we take cars in Jersey,* Lee thought. The Muslims transporting Lee thought it was peculiar, that Lee's level of fear wasn't skyrocketed.

Especially with Lee being an American. But, little did they know, Lee was a man who feared nothing in life, not even death, that no man could stop when it came for anyone.

———

When D'Shawn had finally made it back home from Newark's police precinct at 4:00 AM, he was exhausted. The million questions of his whereabouts and good cop, bad cop interrogation techniques ended the moment he refused to talk. He was a suspect, despite him being the owner of the house. The rowhouse next door was abandoned in bad condition. So there were no neighbors. When the detectives requested his DNA samples, he willingly gave it to them, and left the station. He was nowhere near being the killer, so he had nothing to worry about. Putting his key into the door and quietly easing inside his suite, he saw the illumination from the TV in the living room lighting up the darkness of the chilly suite. His first thought was that Varshay had fallen asleep waiting up for him, but when he saw Yalunder balled up in a fetal position, that thought was dismissed.

"What's up Yalunder?"

"Shhh! Don't wake her!" Yalunder said in a loud enough whisper.

This bitch telling me to be quiet in my own shit. This bitch must've fell and bumped her head! D'Shawn thought.

Yalunder had a cover spread covering her lower body, so when she raised up from the sofa with nothing on but her t-shirt and satin thong that were partially see-through, D'Shawn was shocked. *Damn this bitch is gorgeous,* D'Shawn thought. He stood mesmerized as Yalunder sashayed over to him. Looking at the anguish on her face, D'Shawn knew that something was wrong. Yalunder embraced D'Shawn and absentmindedly, he held onto her.

"He left me...right after I graduated. D'Shawn, I was good to him," she whispered as she laid her head on his chest and he rubbed her back for comfort.

"Sorry to hear that, Yalunder," D'Shawn retorted.

But I'm not Dr. Love, baby girl! D'Shawn thought.

"I've been waiting on you to come home, she's sleep in there... I put sleeping pills in her drink, pain pills."

What!? I can't believe I'm hearing this conniving shit, thought D'Shawn, shaking his head.

"You what, Yalunder?" D'Shawn asked to make sure that he'd heard her correctly.

"D'Shawn, he wasn't for me, and she's not for you... I could prove it,"

"Yalunder, are you okay?" D'Shawn asked, pulling Yalunder back to look in her eyes for her sanity level. But all that stared back at him was a gorgeous woman that definitely turned him on. He also saw pain, bewilderment, and salaciousness.

"Yes I'm okay, please D'Shawn, just hold me for a while," Yalunder said then wrapped her arms around D'Shawn's neck, bringing him down to her level and kissing him passionately. He wasn't adamant and it made things go smooth for her.

Damn this bitch done busted her move. I knew she was fucked up about me, D'Shawn thought to himself. Her tongue tasted of a sweet wine, and made him want more of her.

"You gave her pain pills?" D'Shawn broke off the passionate kiss, saying.

"Pain pills, baby," Yalunder exclaimed with an impish smile on her face. "Come," she said, grabbing D'Shawn's hand and walking over to the sofa.

Sitting down on the plush leather sofa. She quickly unfastened his belt and let his jeans fall to his ankles. Yalunder was pleased to find D'Shawn already erected. She knew that she was a bad bitch and that D'Shawn wanted her much as she wanted him. She pulled his dick through the slot of his Polo briefs and placed it in her mouth, where she artistically worked her magic with her superb head game.

"Damn!" D'Shawn purred with curled toes. She sucked his dick slow and deep at first, then increased her pace.

"Damn, this shit ain't right," D'Shawn whispered as he pulled back stopping Yalunder.

Nigga, we done crossed the line already! Yalunder thought.

"No, please D'Shawn I need this...Tony P means nothing to me no more and she don't love you like you deserve to be loved."

What the fuck she talking 'bout? D'Shawn thought as he listened attentively.

"If I tell you something, please don't tell her I told you. Use it to your advantage."

"Tell me, I promise I won't tell her shit," D'Shawn said, ready to learn what possible reason that she could give him of why Varshay's love was spurious. Especially with how good he was to Varshay. He'd been told before that what looked good wasn't always good on the inside. *Do I really know Varshay on the inside?* He asked himself introspectively.

"Tell me," D'Shawn said sensing her reluctance.

"She don't love you, D'Shawn. She still talks to T-Mac behind your back and make you believe that she hates him."

"What!" D'Shawn screamed at the bombshell lie.

"Shush! That's why I didn't want to tell you now."

"What the fuck do you mean?!" D'Shawn whispered in a shout.

"I'm not telling you no more until I get some of this dick," Yalunder retorted as she grabbed ahold of D'Shawn's dick and sucked him back to an erection, he was less adamant.

This hoe probably lying! D'Shawn thought as he grabbed a handful of Yalunder's delicate curls and began to fuck her mouth like it was her pussy.

"Damn Yalunder!" he moaned out at the sweet fellation. Yalunder didn't want to spoil him on her superb head game. She wanted to feel him inside her throbbing pussy that soaked her thongs from her juices flowing excessively. Yalunder pulled back abruptly, and got positioned doggy style on the sofa. She slid out of her soaked thong and spread her high yellow ass cheeks apart and her pussy all at once, artistically. The redolence of her sexual arousal was enticing and made D'Shawn's erection stiffer. *Damn, she got a phat ass pussy!* D'Shawn thought as he stared at the mango between Yalunder's legs.

"Fuck me D'Shawn, it's just me and you... no regrets, beat this pussy like you mad!" Yalunder requested.

"No regrets, huh?" D'Shawn exclaimed as he entered Yalunder deeply and powerfully.

"Uhhh! Shit!" Yalunder purred in a gaping whisper. *She don't deserve him, he belonged to me the moment we laid eyes on each other for the first time,* Yalunder thought as D'Shawn thrusted in and out of her wet, tight pussy.

"Yess! D'Shawn, fuck me good! This has always been yo' pussy!" She moaned out simultaneously throwing her pussy back into his strokes.

▭

When Lee had finally made it to his destination, the aggressive hospitality had transformed from a ten to zero. He was now in the presence of the King of Riyadh, who was as well the man he was scheduled to see. His name was King Jihad Mohamad, an old prudent man, who Lee had feasted with lovely. He was introduced to the king's gorgeous daughter named Princess Reem Mohamad. Lee was surprised to learn that despite their accent, they all spoke American English well. Reem was a twenty-one-year-old childless woman, who made it transparent that she held a crush for Lee instantly, the moment she saw him.

At the king's palace on the balcony it was just the two of them, cozily attentive in each other's embrace. He held onto her from behind while staring out at the city and the ardent sun setting. It was beautiful, and unbelievable to Lee that he had the princess of Riyadh in his arms. Last night, she'd crept into his room furtively and demanded for him to make love to her. She wanted it specifically done in the American fashion, and Lee gave it to her at her behest. He fucked her long and hard, and now with three days left, she wanted every moment spent with her. Lee found out that Bobby was her older and only sibling. And that Bobby was a fugitive of Riyadh, who was wanted for killing a noble Prince then fled to America, with the help of his father. Many people believed that Bobby was in a cave underground hidden in a vast city somewhere in Saudi Arabia. Riyadh was where all of the heroin came from, and how Bobby was able to lock down the East Coast with the best heroin.

"Will you come back and stay longer?" Reem asked Lee. She was petite in his arms, standing five-feet-four-inches,125lbs. But under her black Muslim gown she had an ass that was firm and succulent, despite not being enormous. Her flawless dark brown skin had a smooth, delicate scintillation to it. She was the Houri of Riyadh and Lee had become the lucky man.

"Acourse I will be back, and stay longer," Lee retorted.

In fact, he couldn't wait to come back, and kind almost wanted to stay longer than intended. But he had to bridle himself and stay focused on his purpose of coming there in the first place. Unbeknownst to Lee, the real purpose was in his arms, he just couldn't see it yet.

"I will be waiting. You just don't know how good you made love to me. Never have a man do me the way you treated me," Reem exclaimed feeling on Lee's dick from behind her through his Muslim robe.

"The sun is setting, please come to the temple and let me bless you in prayer," Reem recommended.

"I don't know how to Salah the Maghrib yet," Lee retorted.

"I'll do it for you, don't worry," Reem said.

"I will come with you only if you let me make love to you before I leave—" Before he could finish, Reem pulled Lee down and kissed him passionately. The twosome kissed like it was the last day on earth.

"Come now, soon the bell will sound, we can't be late," Reem said as she wrapped her hijab around her beautiful face and head artistically, then took Lee's had in a hastened strut. Downstairs they left they palace and strutted over to the enormous dome temple. Lee, like everyone else, wore a black Muslim gown and sandals. *This shit ain't too bad after all. Salaam alaikum,* Lee thought to himself eager to learn more of the Arabic language. When they got to the temple, they greeted the Arabs at the door, whose job was to guard the temple from suicide bombers or any other threats.

"Salaam alaikum," Lee said to the two guards.

"Wa waikum salaam," Both Muslim guards retorted in unison.

Once inside, the noble princess Reem, sat on a white and gold throne and led more than fifteen hundred other Muslims in the sunset prayer to their God Allah. *Hell yeah, I'll be back. I can't wait to tell D'Shawn 'bout this powerful bitch,* Lee thought.

<hr/>

After hearing the recorded conversation of Varshay and Yalunder, cropped and edit by Yalunder, who used a particular app, where it made Varshay's voice emanate from a texting program. Whatever Yalunder texted to the app, Varshay's voice emanated as if it was Varshay in conversation. D'Shawn's heart had hit the surface and shattered into pieces. Not wanting to face her to hear all the excuses that a woman could possibly come up with, D'Shawn went to clear his mind at his mother and auntie's home.

Sitting in the living room while smoking a purple haze blunt and scrolling through the channels, D'Shawn tried in every possible way to fathom what was the price of real love. His thoughts were vagrant, and his soul, soulless. *I gave the bitch the world and she go 'round my back and continue to fuck with this nigga,* D'Shawn thought as he pulled hard on the blunt and exhaled a thick cloud of smoke. D'Shawn heard footsteps coming down the hall, then saw his mom and auntie appear, who was on her way to work.

"I know I smelled you," D'Shawn's Auntie Marie said.

"Sure," D'Shawn retorted, passing her the swiss blunt, while taking in the transfiguration of his mom. *Damn ma, you getting on the thin side,* D'Shawn thought.

"Good morning ma, are you okay?" he asked his mom who was grabbing the blunt from Marie.

"After I hit this good smellin' weed, I will," Connie retorted, giving everyone a good laugh.

"Child let me go, I'll see y'all later," Marie said, dismissing herself.

"Okay auntie, drive safe," D'Shawn retorted, as the door closed.

"Why you up so early? Alex here, I see?" D'Shawn stated referring to his mother's boyfriend.

"Yeah, the whale back there snoring like always," Connie retorted passing D'Shawn back the blunt.

"Are you exercising mom, looks live you've lost weight?" D'Shawn asked concerned about his mom's health.

"Slim fast boy, I'm trying to catch me a quiet whale. I'm tired of the one back there," Connie said, causing D'Shawn to burst into laughter.

"Boy, that ain't even funny, and why you over here this morning and not in bed with Varshay?"

The look on D'Shawn's face concerned her. He was no longer gladsome-spirited, so she inquired.

"Are y'all okay?"

"Nawl ma, I think I need to continue to search the sea for the right mermaid."

"Boy, what you mean? That girl is beautiful," Connie explained.

"Yeah, but on the inside, she only pretty to herself... she still wants T-Mac."

"Boy, stop it," Connie retorted, followed by a moment of silence. She had her own problems, and the only advice she found soothing to give her hurt son was a mother's genuine comfort.

"C'mere son," Connie exclaimed, taking a seat next to D'Shawn on the sofa, and putting him in her arms like she used to do when he was a little boy.

"Me and your father had the same problem once, D'Shawn," Connie said, resting her head on D'Shawn's shoulder and holding him tight.

"Your dad took me away from my first love and I wasn't over Paul, and D'Shawn knew it as well."

"So how did he handle it?" D'Shawn asked his mom.

"He left me son, until I came back to him," Connie said choking back on tears, remembering her love affair with D'Shawn's father, D'Shawn Hayes.

"What made you come back?" D'Shawn inquired.

Connie laughed and then stated, "Knowing I was a fool to leave a man who loved me for who I was, and took care of me. Just to run back to a man who loved what was between my legs. Son, I was lovin' by myself..." She paused on the verge of tears, but she managed to bridle her emotions for the sake of her son. "Until I found your father," she retorted.

"Thanks mom, you've really helped me make my mind up," D'Shawn said.

"Just be careful son, and speaking of D'Shawn Hayes... a letter came for you."

"My dad wrote me, where is he!?" D'Shawn asked excitedly. He hadn't heard from his father in years. And the last he'd heard was that he was in a federal prison in Atlanta, Georgia, trying to get transferred up north so that he could be closer to home.

"He's in Trenton Federal Penitentiary, and wants to see you," Connie exclaimed putting a smile on D'Shawn's face. "Let me go get the letter," said Connie strutting off to go retrieve the letter that meant so much to her son. While he awaited, he thought about him and Varshay and all the lavishness he now had. He was farther than niggas who'd been in the game all their life. And had enough money put away to get out the game for a while.

After seeing what happened to Juicy and Olivia, D'Shawn was hit with a revelation on the prospect of life. He didn't want to have it all, just for someone to come along and take it from him. Whether a nigga or the Feds, when it was gone he would either be dead or like his father, serving life in the Fed. *I have enough money to promote my own title, maybe J Mack can help me!* D'Shawn thought.

"I could secure my dreams now and pursue it while fuckin' all the hoes I want. Fuck a relationship, a bitch didn't deserve my loyalty. I gave this bitch the world and she still fuck me over," D'Shawn lowly said to himself while searching for the real estate agent Brittney in his phone.

▭

When Varshay awoke, she had extreme cotton mouth and an agitating headache. She was dying for a drink of water. When she looked at the clock next to her bed on a nightstand, she saw that it was 9:00 AM and D'Shawn wasn't in bed with her. *Where the hell is D'Shawn? Leon had left a note saying that he had to handle something and that he would be in late. Not that he wouldn't be home at all,* she thought as she walked into the living room. On her way to the kitchen, she saw Yalunder sitting up on the sofa engrossed in watching "Dragon Ball Z" series.

"Good morning, sleeping beauty," Yalunder said mirthfully. Varshay held up her index finger instructing Yalunder to hold on momentarily, for she was in more need of water than exchanging morning amenities. When Varshay got to the refrigerator, she grabbed a water jug and gulp down a more than sufficient amount. The water gave her life, refreshing her to a better mood.

"Ahhh!" Varshay exhaled, screwing the top back on the jug then securing it back into the refrigerator.

"Now that's what you call refreshing water," she exclaimed, rubbing her temples.

"Now back to your good mood ass, bitch. Good morning to you too. I'm glad to see that you are in a good mood. That wine we had put my ass out... so please tell me why D'Shawn isn't home?" Varshay asked.

"I don't know girl, when a man don't come home, my mama say call the jails first then worry if he not there," said Yalunder.

"Did he at least come in? I thought I heard him," Varshay said while checking her phone for missed calls.

"Nope!" Yalunder answered.

"Great, his phone going to voicemail too," Varshay exclaimed. "So, what do you want to do today?" Varshay asked Yalunder as she climbed underneath the blanket spread with her and joined watching "Dragon Ball Z".

"You still watch this shit... their mouth don't even move?" Varshay asked.

"Bitch, don't hate 'cause Goku look better than D'Shawn's black ass," Yalunder defended her favorite cartoons.

"Whatever bitch," Varshay retorted.

"Anyways... I think I will get rid of Tony P's shit and move on. His loss is my gain. Ain't no sweat in my game," Yalunder said confidently.

"That's what I'm talking about, bitch!" Varshay exclaimed. She was happy to see that her friend was back. "There is always a good man out there who knows how to treat a good woman," Varshay said.

"And fuck them good too," Yalunder retorted, causing Varshay to burst out laughing.

"Bitch, you is crazy!" Varshay exclaimed, missing the compliment of her man's good performance last night between him and her best friend.

CHAPTER 23

"THERE HE IS NOW, baby. Remember, let me do the talkin' and bitch, don't let me catch you clockin' my man," Nicole said to Latoya, as they watched Leon check into the 5-star restaurant, where the best Italian food in Camden, NJ was served.

"Girl I see why you fucked up 'bout that nigga, everything 'bout him screaming money," Latoya exclaimed checking Leon's fresh to death outfit and conspicuous costly jewelry.

"See, you already being a hoe, don't let me tell E-Money," Nicole retorted before Leon made it to the table.

"Hey there ladies," Leon spoke while wrapping his arms around Nicole, and kissing her on the lips.

"Hey baby, I'm glad you made it safe. Leon, this is my sister Latoya, who I've been tellin' you 'bout and Latoya, this is my man Leon."

"You been running me crazy 'bout... we know," Latoya said, putting a stop to the formality of greetings.

"Nice meeting with you, Latoya," Leon said shaking hands with Latoya, and flashing a hypnotic smile. *Damn I see why he got her, this nigga is fine as hell with them sexy ass pearly whites. He could star for Colgate,* Latoya thought.

"Nice meeting you too, Leon" Latoya retorted.

"So did y'all order?" Leon inquired, grabbing the menu in front of Nicole.

"Not yet baby, we wanted to talk first," said Nicole.

"Well damn Cole, at least get something to drink," Leon retorted.

"Umm... we'll wait for that too," Nicole said.

Now she had his undivided attention, and when Leon looked over at Latoya too, he saw that she too wanted to talk judging the look on her face.

"Well damn, let's talk then. Just don't talk me out my draws, 'cause em hungry, B," Leon said causing both women to crack up in laughter.

This nigga is a clown, I like him! Thought Latoya.

"Okay Leon, baby I called you to introduce you to my sister. Umm as you know from when I told you Camden is our city—"

"And we dry on a plug," Latoya said interrupting Nicole who wasn't well with negotiating if it wasn't getting straight to the fucking business. She knew how to mastermind numbers and use her body as a costly price tag, but the drug negotiating was for Latoya. *Damn Latoya is a bad bitch herself,* Leon thought of the gorgeous heavyset woman.

"So what plug we referring to?" Leon asked, frankly.

"We need a faithful line of Mr. Boy and Ms. Becky."

"What type of weight we talkin' 'bout?" Leon asked.

"No fronts, straight up business, twenty kilos of the boy," Latoya exclaimed.

"Twenty?" Leon asked in surprise of the amount that the beautiful heavyset woman was requesting.

"Twenty," Latoya retorted, making herself clear.

"I'mma big girl, so I eat big, feel me," Latoya said smiling, praying that Leon could help her. She waited anxiously for Leon to seal her fate, while he took a moment to contemplate his answer.

"For you, on my baby face, $65,000 apiece. That's the lowest I could get cha on the boy."

"Money isn't a problem, I pay fo' what I ask fo' in full," said Latoya.

"Well that's good, for the Ms. Becky give me 17 flat. They go fo' 18.5, but for you 17 flat," Leon stipulated.

"Great numbers... how soon could we do business?" Latoya asked ready to cure the drought in Camden. Leon looked at his Rolex and saw that sunset was on the way. He had to handle another negotiating deal with a nigga in Harlem after he left Camden.

"How 'bout we set it up for tomorrow. You send Nicole back with the money and I'll send a runner back with her tomorrow when I call for her," Leon stipulated.

"Thank you so much, Leon!" Latoya exclaimed ecstatically.

"You're welcome, now B, can we eat now?" Said Leon, ready to get his grub on and causing both women to erupt in laughter again.

⊏⊐

Varshay was completely torn emotionally and had no understanding to how D'Shawn had been treating her lately. Locking herself in their suite and having sleepless nights from sitting up waiting on him had gotten to be exhausting for her. Yalunder would call her to cheer her up, but it did nothing but reminded her of her reality. D'Shawn was tripping for nothing. Sitting in her tub soaking in cinnamon bubble bath all she could do was cry.

"He tells me he will give me room to get over T-Mac. What the fuck is he talking 'bout and where the fuck did that suddenly come from?" Varshay cried out perplexed of the vicissitude of D'Shawn's state of mind.

"I fucking love this man, T-Mac is nowhere on my mind," Varshay said as she picked up her phone resting on the toilet seat. She called D'Shawn for the umpteenth time, and still got sent to his voicemail. She dared not to text him because he would only text back: "T-Mac"

"I can't believe this shit!" Varshay screamed in furor throwing her phone into the water. D'Shawn had canceled all of her credit cards, and withdrew every dime out of her account. To most women, those were signs to a man moving on.

He's been somewhere else laid up with God know only who for three damn nights, Varshay thought.

"What's going on, I don't understand!" she cried out.

She now wanted to call Yalunder but saw that she no longer had a phone.

"FUCK!" She screamed frustratingly

———

"D'Shawn! Yes! Yes!" Yalunder screamed out in ecstasy as D'Shawn fucked her hard from the back. Her head was buried in the pillows and her ass arched in the air. Breathless, she was from the long hours of consistent lovemaking.

"Baby I feel you in my stomach!" Yalunder yelled out.

SMACK! D'Shawn slapped her on her succulent ass cheeks.

"Yes baby! Yes baby!" Yalunder submissively cried out. D'Shawn was engrossed in his own world, loving every moment that he spent with Yalunder. She had some good pussy and D'Shawn wanted it on every given chance. The moment Varshay dropped Yalunder off home, D'Shawn had pulled up shortly and brought her to his lowkey suite that only two people knew of, and those were his cousins.

"Baby, I'm cumming!" Yalunder screamed climaxing. Her body shook from an electrifying wave of ecstasy as she orgasmed and caused D'Shawn to explode inside her extremely wet pussy.

"Yes baby, yes!" She purred loudly, gripping his dick with her tight pussy walls. *Damn, had I known that this pussy was good like this—* D'Shawn thought.

SMACK!

"Boy, that hurt now!" Yalunder screamed while turning on her back, and pulling D'Shawn down by her stallion thighs. Passionately, they kissed each other. With bodies covered in sweat the duo, just couldn't get enough of each other.

"Umm" Yalunder moaned out.

"No regrets, right?" Yalunder asked, caressing D'Shawn's baby face with her hands, loving the smooth feel of his hairless face. The redolence of their sex was highly in the air and on her hands.

"No regrets," D'Shawn retorted placing his lips on Yalunder's, slowly arousing another erection.

"What will you do 'bout her?" Yalunder asked.

"Give her time to think about what she fucked up. Like I told you ma, I'm done with relationships."

Yeah we'll see, I bet this pussy change yo mind, Yalunder thought.

"As long as you continue to give me this dick, we cool boo, and control our feelings because two people can't keep fuckin' and not catch feelings. It may not matter to you, but I still want you to know you're the only nigga who will be fucking me. I lay down for one, not whomever," Yalunder spoke truthfully, then reached down, grabbing D'Shawn's throbbing dick. She slowly placed him inside her wetness, then gyrated her hips and arched her back as she slammed all of his dick inside of her.

"Oh Jesus!" She exhaled, gasping for air. "D'Shawn!"

———

Lee was back in town, and he was not happy after hearing what had happened with Juicy and Olivia. He and Juicy were homies, and he was one of Lee's sergeants. What really had him fiery and furious was that someone had the audacity to rob them so boldly. He knew the fundamentals of the game and the code in the streets. He had heard D'Shawn and Leon's suspects of who could be behind it. They were playing it humble and prudent by not jumping to conclusions and bringing wrath on 33rd and Santa, T-Mac's turf. Soon someone would pay, because letting it ride was only inviting the next bold mother-fucka to do it. That, Lee knew well. Sitting in Bobby's office drinking on a glass of Hennessy on rocks, Lee was putting an order for more weapons. On the other end, Bobby had some concerns to bring to Lee's attention, to get his feel on the fact that Leon had ordered a large shipment of heroin.

"Lee, your brother asked me to ship him twenty kilos of heroin."

"Twenty, straight up?" Lee asked surprisingly.

"Exactly, now my problem is this, a drop was just made three days ago, and pretty transparently, it's too early for anyone to be ready to reup," Bobby exclaimed skeptically.

"Did he pay for them?" Lee asked, already knowing he answer.

"Yes, he have—"

"Then there's nothin' to worry 'bout Bobby, as long as your end come back, remember?" Lee reminded Bobby of his own stipulations. And not appreciating the skepticism he had for his brother. *But damn Leon, who was getting twenty kilos of heroin?* Lee wanted to know. But as well he had no clue, like Bobby.

"Okay, that erased my concern... how did you enjoy Riyadh?"

"It was great. Can't wait to go back," Lee retorted with a smile, thinking about Reem at the moment.

"I believe you, Reem can't wait herself. Whatever you did to my sister got her wanting to come to America. Just be careful, because she loves differently than these American women... the last dude that hurt her, she strapped a bomb to his ass and tried to send him to space... like a space ship or rocket," Bobby stated, with a straight face.

"I can tell," Lee retorted.

"Well I'll have a shipment to you in a couple days," Bobby said dismissing Lee to attend to an importing meeting. He had visitors from the West Coast ready to finally consolidate business.

"Okay Bobby... just give me a call," Lee said leaving the office.

On his way out the door, he walked up on Bobby's secretary in her black booty shorts and pressed his dick against her nicely firm ass, impertinently. She was startled, but only for a split second.

"When you goin' to let me ride the wave with all this?" Lee asked the brunette while rubbing on her soft ass.

"Whenever you find time to," she responded seductively reaching behind her and gave Lee's dick a squeeze.

"When is your break?" Lee asked her.

"12:30 to 1:30 PM," she retorted. Lee grabbed a pen and paper and quickly wrote his number down.

"Call me so I can make that hour the best hour of your life," Lee said then walked out of the shop to his black-on-black Range Rover. He was so caught up in the sexy brunette's adoration and nimble thoughts of the many positions he would fuck her in come noon, that he never saw the nigga behind the tent in the dark blue Dodge Durango watching his every move. He was too checking the brunette out, but had other intentions for her, other than a good fuck.

Bean and Chase had the block back in control and their clientele in Harlem satisfied. The hit on D'Shawn's trap helped them smooth things out with their future plans. T-Mac was laying low from the streets, trying to heal from the painful bite wound, while being nursed by Tracy who was sexually exhausting him.

"Blood, why don't you take yo' ass to the doctor, maybe that hoe had something?" Bean asked T-Mac who sat on the leather sofa smoking on a purple haze blunt.

"Man, I told you B, I don't do doctors," T-Mac retorted blowing a ring of smoke in the air.

"Okay nigga, when your neck fall off, that's your ass!" Said Chase at the minibar sitting on a stool drinking on a glass of Remy. They were all at T-Mac's suite.

"Ain't that nigga Tony P thowin' a party at the Morosa tonight?" T-Mac asked, wincing in pain.

"It's all over Facebook, and it seems that ya girl and D'Shawn have finally parted ways."

"What!" T-Mac screamed, regretting letting Bean and Chase see his overreacting love bound, that had him out of character. But it was no secret of how in love he was.

"Yeah man, see it for yourself," Chase said, pulling up Varshay's page on Facebook revealing her status as single.

Damn I gotta get my bitch back, T-Mac thought.

"I wonder what happen... shit looked content with them," T-Mac exclaimed.

"There you go, a chance to get ya bitch back. You know what they say. The nigga who bust that cherry will always be able to hit that," Bean said.

"You think she'll be at the party tonight?" T-Mac asked.

"I think she will be Blood. Her girl Yalunder's fine ass will definitely be in there with Tony P," said Bean.

"Yo, B, I'mma step in that bitch tonight," T-Mac said determinedly

—

Tracy sat in the room and heard every word that T-Mac and his homies had conversed. *So, he thinks I'm something to play with. Nigga, we have a baby together and one that you can't deny!* Tracy thought angrily. Her and T-Mac had no stipulations on a relationship. But it was transparent that they deserved mutual respect for each other. Their intimacy was developing into a relationship where expectations of fidelity became inevitable. *I never showed my ass 'bout a nigga fuckin' another bitch. Because what a nigga could do, a bitch could do better. But I will not let this bitch step in the way of me and T-Mac!* Tracy thought placing her earbuds to her iPad back into her ear to hear Beyoncé's song "Drunk in Love".

CHAPTER 24

D'SHAWN SAT in the barber chair in Mr. Miley's shop on 110th and Virginia, waiting patiently for the old man to finish up with a customer. Despite him avoiding Varshay on every corner, he'd found himself missing her in every aspect that Yalunder couldn't fulfill. Her unique smile and laugh had made a difference to him in his life. Last night he'd crept in the suite and found her asleep in his t-shirt and Polo boxers, never noticing his presence. The feeling he had when he stuck the key in the door, had ill-humored him at the prospect of walking into his own home to find Varshay in bed with another man.

It's crazy how the mind can inflame a person's train of thoughts, D'Shawn thought ignoring another text from Varshay, but responding back to Yalunder's. *It's fucked up how hoes cut throated each other, one of the main reasons why I can't trust 'em,* he thought while reading Yalunder's text.

Yalunder: *Hey boo are you goin' to Tony P's party, just curious?*

Now she know I'mma go attend the party, what kind of question is that? D'Shawn thought, texting Yalunder back.

D'Shawn: *Yeah, I will be in there tonight why you asked?*

Yalunder: *Because, I need me some dick daddy...I miss you* 😞

Every time you fuck these hoes good they want to lock a nigga down. I tried that shit and got made a fool out of, D'Shawn thought, so engrossed in his phone texting Yalunder back that he never heard the sound bells off on the door indicating that another customer had entered the shop for service.

D'Shawn: *Ma look here, I will be home tonight. You have a key, let yourself in and I will see you after the club.*

"So, you can sit up here and text the next bitch but don't want to answer any of my calls, texts, or bring your ass home!" Varshay spat after snatching D'Shawn's phone out his hands in the midst of him texting Yalunder.

Damn this bitch just rolled on me! D'Shawn thought while looking from Mr. Miley to Varshay.

"Son, I had no clue she was here for you," Mr. Miley said shrugging his shoulders up and down.

"Please Mr., stay out of this," said Varshay feeling the vibration of D'Shawn's phone, alerting on an incoming text. "Why D'Shawn? What the fuck have I done to make you assume that T-Mac is of any of my concerns? I fuckin' love you and you want to find an excuse to be out and 'bout. Today I need answers, not tomorrow, or the next day after!" Varshay screamed in a raging fit.

"Excuse me miss, but can y'all take y'alls problem outside? I don't mean any disrespect if I sound stern. It's just I have too much to lose if a quarrel breaks out. This shop is my life," Mr. Miley spoke calmly and peace minded.

"Sorry sir, I understand," Varshay said to Mr. Miley then looked back at D'Shawn, whose eyes were on the phone in her hands. "I'll be outside."

"Varshay, give me my phone girl!" D'Shawn shouted as he leaped out the barber chair taking off behind Varshay who hastily stormed out the door, then fucked his world up when she pressed her back against the door, preventing D'Shawn from coming out. The phone vibrating in her hand again had prompted her to do the move in the first place.

"Varshay! Get off the door!" D'Shawn screamed from inside,

pushing at the door, but her Jordan's were planted in the concrete making the door adamant to moving her. Varshay looked at D'Shawn's phone and lost her breath when she saw Yalunder's name appearing on an incoming text.

"Yalunder!" Varshay shouted frantically.

Please let this be some kind of coincidence that he's seeing another Yalunder and not my Yalunder, she thought. But it was evident by the number that she knew well, that it was her Yalunder.

"Varshay get off the damn door, woman!" D'Shawn continued to scream as Varshay opened the text from no other than her best friend.

Yalunder: *I'mma be a good girl and be waiting on you when you come in. I'm not Varshay, I know how to appreciate mine... my dick!*

"I cannot believe this bitch!" Varshay screamed as her heart rate accelerated to the peak of a panic attack. Unconsciously, her weight slid off the door and D'Shawn quickly stormed out the door staring at Varshay's back.

"Varshay let me get my phone!" he said.

SMASH!

"Bitch, are you crazy!" D'Shawn shouted as he watched Varshay just shatter his phone to the concrete and stomp on it for good measure, then turn to face him with tears cascading down her face in a flood.

"You got plenty money to be fuckin' my friend. I'm sure that you'll be able to pay for a new phone. D'Shawn you can't pay for love, but there's a way to pay for betrayal. I let T-Mac fuck me over, now it's you. I took a chance and gave you my all. For you to come out of nowhere with this T-Mac shit—"

"Varshay, you know what you did. Bitch, you—"

SMACK!

"Call me another bitch!" Varshay screamed after slapping D'Shawn with all of her womanly force.

"Whatever she told you, I just hope that it was worth it," Varshay said with tears cascading down her face and her entire body shaking so badly that you could hear her teeth rattling.

Damn she's hurt! D'Shawn thought.

"Varshay...c'mere," D'Shawn said, reaching out to grab Varshay for comfort, in an attempt to ease her pain.

"Don't touch me!" she yelled backing away from him.

"I would never betray you, that's why it hurt me so much to see you accuse me of still fuckin' with T-Mac. Fuck you and T-Mac!" Varshay exclaimed then stormed off.

All D'Shawn could do was watch her leave in the Range Rover he'd got her for graduation. Though she was gone, the pain still lingered. The pain of hurting her had left a whole in his heart. For the first time, he'd realized that he was being selfish by not sitting down and talking things out with Varshay, and concluding logical inferences.

If she truly loved that nigga T-Mac, then she would've ran back to the nigga like mama ran back to my dad. The door was open and I let her friend walk right through it, D'Shawn thought as he walked back into the shop to get his regular haircut for the club tonight. He would deal with Varshay later, when she was in the right state of mind.

▭

Varshay was devastated from the heart-breaking revelation of D'Shawn and Yalunder.

"How could she do me like this and supposed to be my home-girl?" Varshay cried out wiping her tears away from her eyes while accelerating absentmindedly, 60mph in a 45mph speeding zone.

"I fucking loved this man more than myself and he was too blind to see it!" Varshay yelled out hysterically while punching in Yalunder's phone number into her new iPhone.

"Bitch pick up, now!" Varshay shouted out. When she pressed the send button, her phone fell from her fumbling, trembling hands, and unto the driver's floor.

"Shit!" she exclaimed, reaching below her, partially looking over the dashboard while feeling for her iPhone on the floor. She was too low to see that she was in the midst of running a red light at an inter-section and unable to break on time as she went head on with an eigh-teen-wheeler semi-truck.

"Noo!" All that could be heard was the screeching tires of the Range Rover, and the impact of the deadly collision.

Urrrrk! Boom! Varshay having on no seat belt, was feeble at defeating death as she was ejected from the Range Rover, going through the windshield.

CHAPTER 25

"Yess T-Mac, uhh shit!" Tracy moaned out as T-Mac thrusted in and out of her tight asshole. After finally deciding on whether she was ready to give her all to him, by allowing him to penetrate her anally, she fucked him good to exhaustion, and allowed him to lick her asshole thoroughly until it was sufficiently lubricated. When she guided him into her back door, the ultimate question came from him.

"Are you ready fo' that?"

When she responded, "the question is for you to answer," T-Mac gave it to her slowly and gently.

Now they were both in bliss as he entered her deeply. Seeing his dick expand her asshole and how she artistically used her muscles made him cum instantly inside her.

"Argghh!" he groaned.

"Yess! Yes!" Tracy shouted, coming to an orgasm as well. Both exhausted, T-Mac collapsed on top of Tracy, causing her to burst into laughter. "Boy get off me so I can shower," Tracy shouted.

"You fucked up 'bout me, huh?" T-Mac asked.

"I wouldn't have gave my baby daddy the ass if I wasn't."

Baby daddy? T-Mac thought perplexed.

"Yo what... Baby daddy?" T-Mac inquired.

"Yes T-Mac...we're having a baby."

"Get the fuck out of here!" T-Mac exclaimed excited and surprisingly.

"No games, I came up positive and last I checked I've only been fucking one nigga, let alone unprotected and I really... got feelings for him. Something he need to see and move on from what's not meant," Tracy said as she rolled out of bed and proceeded to walk to the bathroom, leaving T-Mac speechless. *Damn I'm 'bout to be a father!* He thought as he watched Tracy's undulations, then her stop in mid-stride.

"Are you comin to shower with us?" Tracy asked while looking back at T-Mac spreading her ass apart, revealing the semen that he'd released in her.

"It's so wet, daddy," she retorted.

This bitch looks just like Roxy Reynolds when she does that shit. Man, I'm 'bout to be a dad, T-Mac thought, then made his mind up not giving up the opportunity to fuck Tracy in her ass again. He was hood.

"Hell yeah, I'm coming to shower," T-Mac exclaimed hopping from bed to join his baby mama in a much-needed shower. Tracy's plan was working right into the disappointment that lay ahead for them both, unbeknownst.

SMACK!

"Boy stop slapping my ass like that!" Tracy exclaimed, turning around softly hitting T-Mac in his nicely toned chest.

"You know you like that shit," T-Mac retorted, embracing Tracy in his arms, then kissed her passionately on her lips. When she opened her mouth and their tongues collided, both of them enjoyed the taste of their bodily fluids from love making.

"I want to work on the next step, let's be a family," Tracy said looking T-Mac in his eyes. "I want it to be us," she said rubbing his chest. "No sidekicks. You been the only nigga in this pussy, and you've been fuckin' me like you my man. Now we're forced with a responsibility and I don't believe in abortions. If there's any doubts, please let me know, because we could get a blood test—"

"Ma, I got you, B. There's no need to speak nonsense. And either on that is more understood left unsaid rather than uttered," T-Mac said to Tracy. "I been thinking the same thing."

Lying ass nigga, you goin' to the party tonight to try getting yo' bitch back while she is up for grabs, Tracy thought.

"Do you mean that, T-Mac?" she asked while caressing his dick and arousing him to another erection.

"If I said it baby, then I meant it," T-Mac retorted. Tracy kissed his lips then trailed her tongue down his body until she came face-to-face with his throbbing dick. T-Mac flexed his dick twice and Tracy caught it with her mouth and no hands.

"Damn, baby!" he exhaled a climaxing sigh as his baby mama sucked his dick like a lollipop. *This my dick!* she thought unaware of the ossification in their path, and it wasn't Varshay.

———

Tony P was a couple hours away from celebrating his going away party at Club Morosa. As he laid back getting his dick sucked by a white girl name Kylie, who strongly resembled Miley Cyrus and who as well received a scholarship to the University of Miami, he thought of how far he'd came, and how hard he'd worked to make his family proud of him. When he thought of Yalunder, he was hit with an overwhelming sense of guilt. *When shit was hard for me, it was her standing by my side, and seeing me get through my hardship,* Tony P thought. He hated how the break up went, but for Tony P life goes on.

Since leaving Yalunder, Tony P hadn't heard any more from her. She seemed to be taking the break up far better than he'd thought she would. *She was emotionally destroyed the last time I saw her in this very room,* Tony P thought while cumming.

"Arghhh!" Tony P groaned as he shot his load into Kylie's mouth, who pulled his dick out and stroked the remaining load all over her face.

"Ummm Tony P," Kylie moaned out simultaneously stroking Tony P and licking the tip of his dick.

"Baby I have to give it to you, you're the best!!" Tony P complimented breathlessly, from the superb head game that Kylie had just put down on him

Knock! Knock! Knock!

When Tony P heard the knocks at his front door, he looked at the time on his digital clock on the nightstand and saw that it was only 7:45 PM. *Who the fuck is that?* Tony P wanted to know. He'd told Peanut to meet him at the club and hadn't expected the limousine that he'd rented to show until 10 o'clock.

"Company?" Kylie asked, puzzled as well.

"No, but whoever it is 'bout to—"

Knock! Knock! Knock!

"Yo, who the fuck is it!" Tony P yelled at the persistent knocker at his door.

"I'll be in the shower," Kylie said strutting towards the bathroom.

Damn, deep pussy, good head game, but no ass at all, Tony P thought at the sight of Kylie's flat bottom.

"I'm comin'!" Tony P yelled while putting on his briefs and gym shorts.

Bare-chested, he walked to the front door of his suite. When the knocks came again, Tony P exploded.

"Motherfucka, didn't I say that I was comin'!" Tony P yelled, disregarding looking through the peephole to see whom the visitor was.

"What the fuck!" he yelled, surprised to see the visitor at his front door. She stood there with her hands behind her back and tears cascading down her face. His heart was in commiseration, but there was nothing that could possibly be said to soothe the pain that he'd caused her. When she smiled he became perplexed, and thought about all the psychopath bitches he'd seen after bad breakups.

What the fuck is she smiling for? Tony P thought.

"Tony, do you remember the first rose you gave me?" she asked.

Yeah it was in the gym in the 9th grade when I told my niggas that I would get her number, he remembered.

"Yeah, I do," Tony retorted.

"Well I want to remind you of that rose and the significance of that rose and how it made me feel so special..." she said, while bringing one of her hands from behind her back with a red rose.

Damn! Tony thought. Seeing how hurt she was made him wonder whether he was making the right choice leaving her.

"Here," she said handing Tony the rose with one hand still behind her back.

"I never loved a man the way I love you, Tony. I wanted a family of our own," she paused, choking on her tears that had a perpetual stream flowing down her beautiful face. "I even told you that I would move to Miami with you."

"Tony!" a woman voice screamed from inside. She already knew that he had company which only made matters worse for them both.

"So, you ditched me for Barbie, huh?" she asked Tony, trembling badly.

"Look, we done Yalunder. I'm movin' on so—"

"I know you are," she said, coming from behind her back with a Glock .19 aimed at Tony's head.

Boom! Boom! Boom! Boom! She swiftly stepped back and pulled the trigger four times. Hearing the screams of the white woman she knew from school, she stepped over Tony's lifeless body and walked into the room where she saw Kylie screaming hysterically in a corner with nowhere to go.

"Pleasee Yalunder, nooo!" Kylie screamed as Yalunder aimed at her head.

"You have some raw skills on the court, maybe they got a basketball team where you're going," Yalunder said to the female basketball point guard star, who was on her way to play ball in college at the University of Miami.

"Please Yalunder, he told me."

Boom! Boom! Boom! Yalunder pulled the trigger and splattered Kylie's brains all over the walls in the corner she'd trapped herself in. Yalunder walked back to Tony's body and aimed at his forehead.

"You left me for a Barbie, nigga!" *Boom! Boom! Boom!*

"A nigga always got to bring the hood out a bitch!" Yalunder said as she turned on her heels, leaving both of her victims lifeless with all their lustful thoughts on the plush white carpet, and bedroom walls. Before exiting the suite, she pulled a black skully that rested on her head lower down her face, partially, and evaded the scene. As she drove in her new Range Rover that D'Shawn had bought her, she serenaded to the lyrics of Mary J Blige's song "No More Tears" that emanated from her system.

"I'm not gon' shed no tears!" She sang as her final tears for Tony P cascaded down her face.

The Vice President of Arrigo Benz had just got out of an important meeting with another Vice President of a car dealership from Trenton, NJ. It was 9:00 PM and he wouldn't be clocking out until quarter to 10 o'clock. *Thank God, I can finally get this project on the way,* he thought of his successful results of getting Trenton to compromise business on their clientele. When he got in his office, he loosened up his tie, expecting to relax until he had to clock out. The only people still in the building were him and his mistress secretary, Ms. Linda Hilary. She was a beautiful blonde in her early thirties, who resembled the British model Lily Donaldson. As soon as he sat down in his comfortable plush president chair, his mistress was buzzing him on his intercom.

"Damn Linda, what?" he exclaimed as he looked at the flashing red light on his ornate desk embellished with family photos.

"What's up, Linda?" he asked as he rubbed the fatigue from his eyes while closed.

"Sorry to tell you Mr. Lewis, but your daughter—"

"What about my daughter?" Mr. Lewis asked, alert.

"You're to call a Detective Holmes at 201 225 4583 first."

"Thank you, Linda," Mr. Lewis said as he punched the numbers on his office phone, disconnecting the intercom connection between him and Linda.

The phone rang twice before someone picked up.

"Hello, this is Detective Holmes from the—"

"This is Mr. Lewis, I'm calling 'bout my daughter!" Mr. Lewis exclaimed in panic.

"Sir, I'm sorry to tell you, but earlier today your daughter, Varshay Lewis, was involved in a fatal car accident."

"Nooo! Pleaseee! God nooo!" Mr. Lewis cried out, then collapsed to the floor, going into a massive heart attack. The last thing he saw before his world went dark was the beautiful smile his daughter had, that always warmed his heart.

CHAPTER 26

WHEN E-MONEY SAW that Bobby was closing the shop by letting down the first garage gate to the auto shop, where the rims were installed, he made an inconspicuous exit from the Dodge Durango. He looked at his Hublot watch, and saw that it was shortly after 9PM.

"Perfect timing," he mumbled to himself as he approached Bobby descending the second garage gate.

"Sorry sir, but we are now closed," Bobby said in a deep Arabic accent.

"No Bobby, you have an important meeting."

WOP! E-Money, with agility, delivered an unexpected round house kick to Bobby's jaw, knocking him out cold before he hit the deck.

When E-Money saw that he was snoring, he prided himself of his martial arts techniques and closed the third and last garage gate. From under his black leather jacket, he pulled out his .44 Magnum, and called for the beautiful brunette.

"Yo Emily, help! Bobby just passed out!" E-Money shouted.

"What!?" Emily exclaimed as she came through the side door of the shop, leading into the back lobby.

When she saw Bobby on the ground, and the man standing over him, with his back to her, she rushed to Bobby's aid.

"Oh my gosh, Bobby are you—" *Whack!*

Before she'd made it to him, E-Money turned around swiftly and rammed the butt of his .44 Magnum to her temple, sending her unconsciously to the deck as well.

"I love this shit!" E-Money exclaimed as he pulled out his Trac-Fone and called Latoya on her TracFone.

"What's up baby?" Latoya answered.

"Call them dogs to come pick up this trash." E-Money disconnected the call.

"I wish that I could have fun with you baby, but unfortunately not this time," E-Money said to Emily's unconscious body on the floor

———

The party wouldn't be occurring until after 12 o'clock and T-Mac saw that he had enough time to check up on a couple traps to see how they've been holding up on product and to most definitely check upon his cash.

"Yo Tracy, I'll be back, be ready when I come back!" T-Mac shouted to Tracy who was in the bedroom embellishing herself for the party. She'd finally got T-Mac to let her come along, despite him trying to put his foot down. She was prohibited from any such alcohol whatsoever. T-Mac was definite taking her pregnancy seriously.

"Okay, I'll be ready!" Tracy retorted.

T-Mac grabbed his keys from the bar counter then walked out of the suite in his True Religion outfit ad red Polo snapback fitted cap.

"Damn!" T-Mac winced in pain at the badly deteriorating bite wound on the back of his neck. Despite Tracy cleaning the wound daily to her best ability, the wound had become infected and was threating T-Mac's life, unbeknownst to him. When he made it to the parking lot and put his key into the door of his new Audi Q7, he was swarmed and surrounded by men in black gear with M16 rifles aimed at him.

What the fuck!? T-Mac thought startled.

"Get the fuck down on the ground!!" More than five of them yelled, ready to shoot on sight, but they'd been told specifically not to.

"What the fuck!" T-Mac exclaimed with his hand extended in the air.

"Down or we will shoot. NWPD, get down now!!" They continued to shout at him as he slowly immersed to his knees, putting his hands behind his head. The moment T-Mac's knees hit the pavement, a strong hand took ahold of his arm and brought it behind his back, simultaneously slapping on a pair of cuffs.

"Mr. Troy Mitchell, you are under arrest for the murder of Olivia Johnson and Dominique Preston," Detective David Morris said to T-Mac. As Detective Morris brought T-Mac to his feet, he frisked him and retrieved T-Mac's Glock .40

"You're not leaving home without it, huh?" Morris asked T-Mac who remained quiet. T-Mac knew the street protocol, and that was to never say anything to the jakes. When Detective Morris read T-Mac his constitutional rights, all he could think about was the wound on the back of his neck.

"T-Mac... ain't that what they call you? Son, DNA is like numbers. When it's right, it can never go wrong. I hope you know fundamentals to doing life in prison," Detective Morris said as he closed the back door to the unmarked Yukon.

"Dammit!" T-Mac yelled alone in the back seat, with the rough reality that he may not ever see the streets again.

———

When Tracy heard the knocks at the door, she thought that it was T-Mac locked out at first. Until, she remembered his awareness of the hidden key in the mailbox, that only needed the three-digit passcode to access the lock. She was fumbling with her gold elephant earrings when she grew impatient at the irksome knocking. *Damn, I know that ain't T-Mac's ass knockin' like he done lost his mind,* she thought as she strutted over to the door in her five-inch Jason Wu red stilettos. She instinctively looked through the peephole and saw a very attractive woman with a pretty brown skin complexion. *What the hell? I know he don't have hoes popping up on him. This hoe 'bout to get checked, fo' real!* Tracy thought angrily as she came out her stilettos, ready to pounce, then opened the door.

"May I help you?" Tracy said with an attitude, then quickly realized that she was staring at an undercover detective, judging by the gun and badge on her hip.

"Yes ma'am, are you Tracy Miller?" Detective Michele Cummings asked.

"Yes... that's me. Now, what seems to be the problem?" Tracy asked perplexed.

"Ms. Miller, we're going to ask you nicely to come down to the station for questioning," Detective Cummings said sternly with authority.

"What the fuck y'all need to see me for?" Tracy asked impishly.

"Ms. Miller your boyfriend just got arrested for two murders."

"Oh my God! Noo!" Tracy exclaimed.

"If you're not involved, then we need to know, and we have questions to ask you about Tyrone Stany. You called 911 and reported that you were concerned that something—"

"Man, I don't know shit—" Before she could finish, Tracy was tackled and restrained to the floor by a strong Detective Cummings, and placed in cuffs.

"Tracy Miller, you're under arrest for battery on a law enforcement agent."

"Bitch, you lying!" Tracy spat hysterically.

"Shut up, hoe. I gave your stupid ass a shot," Cummings said with her knee on Tracy's face, pinning her to the ground.

Bitch I got all night to fuck you up! Cummings thought. Behind her came her back up that she'd requested to stay out of sight while she brought Tracy into custody. Being that it was protocol to back her up, her fellow officers were there to back her up.

———

This shit crazy out here B, where the fuck is Leon at? D'Shawn asked Lee on his phone as he drove towards his low-key suite in West Orange NJ to lay low from the streets.

"Man, last time I heard fat boy, he was doin' business with them twenty boys," Lee retorted.

"Man, I can't believe this shit, B!" D'Shawn exclaimed, furious.

The news of Tony P's death was everywhere. Despite D'Shawn fucking his ex and never coming clean about it, D'Shawn saw Tony as a homeboy. It took him hours to get a new phone and the same number after finally recalling his twelve-digit passcode.

"Yo B, who you think did that shit?" D'Shawn asked Lee.

"Man, the same niggas that robbed us" Lee retorted.

"Come on nigga, be realistic, they just picked T-Mac up," D'Shawn retorted.

"And they found Tony P and the white bitch before they arrested him, too," Lee retorted.

"When I see Bean, we might as well—"

"We don't even have to talk about that, we know that he dead," D'Shawn said.

"Shit, he knows that, B," Lee retorted.

"Yo B, hold on. Varshay's mom is callin' me," D'Shawn told Lee when he saw the incoming call from Mrs. Lewis.

"No nigga, call me when you get to the suite," Lee retorted.

"Okay I'll do that, call Leon and tell his ass to get off the streets," D'Shawn said, then clicked over to speak with Mrs. Lewis.

"Hello?"

"D'Shawn baby, where are you!?" Mrs. Lewis cried out.

"What's good ma, why you crying? I'm 'bout to be in the area.

You don't sound too well, are you okay?" D'Shawn asked his mother-in-law, who sounded out of shape.

"D'Shawn, Varshay is dead," Mrs. Lewis cried out.

What did she just say? D'Shawn thought as he pulled over to the side of the road. *Mothers don't play death games,* he thought.

"Mrs. Lewis run that by—"

"Varshay is dead, D'Shawn. Earlier today she was in a fatal car accident..."

"Ma, please stop playin' like that!" D'Shawn screamed, knowing that Mrs. Lewis wouldn't play in such a manner. He didn't know of any compassionate, loving, and caring mother like Mrs. Lewis that would. At that moment, everything became incoherent to D'Shawn.

"My baby gone, D'Shawn!" Mrs. Lewis cried out, along with D'Shawn, whose world had just been turned upside down. *Varshay is dead,* he thought as the inevitable tears fell from his eyes.

The moment when he was seriously considering on working things out with Varshay, had come hours ago, the last time he'd seen her with all the pain on her face. Now he was left with the loss of her and their memories.

"Lord why!" D'Shawn cried out, laying his head on the steering wheel weeping like never before.

***

"Drive safe. Are you sure you don't want me to ride back with you?" Leon asked Nicole as he closed the door to her black-on-black Maybach. They were at a public park in west Newark where Leon had just delivered Nicole the twenty kilos of heroin in three duffel bags.

"Baby relax, I will call you when I get home, or if there are any problems along the way," Nicole said, caressing Leon's stubbly face with her delicate hands.

"You spoil me too much and are overprotective. Remember, don't let this pussy and thongs fool you. I've been doin' this longer than you, and harder than a lot of niggas," Nicole said, then kissed Leon passionately. Behind her was her driver in a black Suburban with the twenty kilos of heroin stashed away safely in a secret compartment in the rear of the SUV.

"Call me when you get there," Leon said.

"I will, baby," Nicole retorted as she rolled up the window to the Maybach, then pulled off, vanishing into the night. *Damn that bitch got me hooked*, Leon thought.

———

So you want to cut me off because of Bently's incarceration, then lie to me 'bout getting out the game, huh?" Latoya asked Bobby who was bound to a chair in her basement at the mansion. With brass knuckles, she'd been beating Bobby's face to complete deformity trying to get him to reveal to her his connect and answer her questions. But despite the torture, he was not breaking. She'd mutilated Emily in front of him, and still tenaciously, he wasn't breaking.

"Fuck you Toya, I'll see you in hell!" Bobby said through clenched teeth, unable to operate his broken jaw.

I'm trippin... this is a damn Sunni Muslim! Latoya thought. Tired and exhausted she removed her Glock .19 from her waistline, and shoved the gun in Bobby's mouth.

"Arghhh!" Bobby winced in pain as the gun parted his jaw and bypassed his toothless swollen, bloody gums.

"I guess we will see each other in hell!" Latoya said, then pulled the trigger.

BOOM! BOOM! The close impact caused a portion of Bobby's brain to fly out the back of his head with a splatter of blood caused by the hollow point slugs.

"Salaam alaikum," Latoya said in Arabic.

"That makes two of us out the game," she retorted, creating a new heroin king, unbeknownst to her. One that would make her reconsider leaving the game for good. Lee.

THE CORTEGE to the gravesite was the most painful part of the funeral, because nobody has ever come back from the grave, when put in the ground. D'Shawn was a wreck but was supported by his family through the entire funeral, showing their respects for Varshay and to give their genuine, condolences to her mother, who was suffering a double tragedy of two of her loved ones. Her daughter was dead at eighteen years old, and her husband hospitalized in critical condition from a massive heart attack.

D'Shawn sat in the limousine with Mrs. Lewis who reminded him so much of Varshay and who'd aged since Varshay's death. Behind them was a Trenton Department of Corrections transport van with Varshay's brother Boo, who was blessed to be permitted to attend the funeral. In front of them in the black hearse laid in a pink casket peacefully, was both of their true love. Connie had declined to go to the gravesite, because she wanted to get home to cook dinner for the family. It was his mom who'd caught all his tears and held him through the funeral. *Why does love have to hurt and why do it have to affect you the most when the person is gone?* D'Shawn wanted to know as he looked out the window and wiped a tear away.

Yesterday, he'd attended Tony P's funeral. His going away had made a record at the Church of God on 12th and M.L.K. The person who you thought would have been the first to show their respects after his family, wasn't present, which a lot of people paid attention to. Yalunder's absence had a lot of people feeling skeptical, including D'Shawn. *She came to Varshay's funeral, the friend she'd betrayed, but not her ex's,* D'Shawn thought.

"Are you okay, D'Shawn?" Asked Yalunder sitting across from him and Mrs. Lewis, as if she could read his mind.

"Yeah, I'm okay," D'Shawn lied.

―――

She hated funerals because it reminded her of what she would soon be faced with, before it was her time to go. She was afraid of death and had no choice but to accept it. Living now with full blown AIDS went beyond anguish and torment. Feeling dismal and in pain, she knew of only one friend that could assuage her pain.

"Where the fuck is my lighter?" she asked herself. When she found her Bic lighter, she prepared the heroin to a liquid form, then transferred it into a dirty syringe needle. Opening and closing her hand to find a bulging vein, she was happy to see her favorite one appear.

"There you go," she said, elated.

Soon there will be no more pain, she thought as she injected the heroin into her veins. As she felt the heroin flow through her veins while lying in her bed, her heart began to accelerate at a rapid pace, which was unusual for her.

"Damn, no pain... no pain," she mumbled in a sluggish state.

She began to sweat excessively and could hear every thump of her heart. As she faded away, she began to convulse violently, while foaming excessively from her mouth. Flapping like a fish out of water, she rolled from the bed and landed on her neck, breaking it instantly. She continued to go into convulsions while gagging on her own tongue. A minute later, she had completely locked up and stopped breathing, after choking to death on her own tongue. She would never feel no pain ever again. Ms. Connie Jenkins was dead on arrival at only age forty-seven years old.

The end